Beyond

HORACIO QUIROGA

Beyond

Translated from the Spanish by Elisa Taber

an object by
SUBLUNARY EDITIONS
of Seattle, WA

Translation copyright © 2022 Elisa Taber

ISBN 978–1–955190–37–4
LCCN 2022943803

All rights reserved. Except for brief passages quoted in a review, regardless of medium, no part of this book may be reproduced in any form or by any means, electronic or mechanical, including photocopying and recording, or by any information storage and retrieval system, without permission in writing from the Publisher.

Manufactured in the United States of America
Printed on acid-free paper

Design and typesetting by Joshua Rothes

Typeset in Linotype Sabon Next and Din Pro

CONTENTS

3	Beyond
15	The Vampire
45	The Flies
49	The Express Train Conductor
63	The Call
71	The Son
78	Lady Lioness
84	The Puritan
93	His Absence
126	Beauty and the Beast
140	Twilight
151	Translator's Note: Grazing Earth

BEYOND

Beyond

I was desperate—the voice continued. My parents definitively denied my feelings for him and had become cruel. The last days, they forbid me appearing on the threshold. Before, I would see him for an instant standing on the corner, waiting for me since morning. Then, not even that.

The week before the prohibition, I asked mother:

"What do you see in him that makes you torture me? Tell me what you know of him. Why is he unworthy of stepping into our house, of visiting me?"

Mother did not answer but asked me to leave. Father grabbed my arm as he entered and, upon hearing what mother said I said, pushed me by the shoulder blade out of the living room door.

"Your mother is wrong. She meant to say that we... Are you listening? She meant to say that we prefer to see you dead than in the arms of that man. Not another word about this."

"Alright," I answered turning paler, I think, than the tablecloth. "I'll never speak of him to you again."

I entered my room slowly and profoundly surprised, surprised to feel myself walk and to see what I saw, because I had decided to die at that moment.

To die! Die in order to rest from that quotidian hell.

Hell was knowing him two steps away, waiting to see me, suffering more than me. I still ask myself: Why would father never consent to me marrying Luis? What did he see in him? He was poor. We were as poor as him.

Oh! I learnt of father's obstinacy, came to know it as well as mother.

"Dead a thousand times," he would say, "before giving her away to that man."

But what did father give me in return? The misfortune of loving wholly, knowing myself loved and condemned not to reach the threshold to see him, not even for an instant.

Dying was preferable, yes. Dying together.

I knew he was capable of killing himself… And I? I, the one that lacked the strength to fulfill her fate alone, would choose death by his side a thousand times over the desperation of never seeing him again.

I wrote him a letter, admitting that I would do anything. A week later, we met at the prearranged place, and occupied one room in the same hotel.

I did not feel proud of what I was about to do or happy to die. It felt fatal, frantic, unrelenting. As though my grandparents, my great grandparents, and my childhood, my first communion, my dreams were exhumed from the past. As though all this served no other purpose but that of impelling me to suicide.

We did not feel happy, I say it again, to die. We abandoned life because she had abandoned us, impeded us from being meant for each other. In the finality and purity of our first embrace, dressed and wearing shoes on our deathbed as we were when we arrived, I understood, touched by joy in his arms, how great my happiness would have been if I had become his girlfriend, his wife.

We took the poison at the same time. During that brief lapse between grasping the glass and bringing it to my lips, the force, my grandparents, that impelled me towards death now appeared by the wayside of fate to restrain me… Too late. Suddenly, the noises that filled the street, the entire city, ceased. They retreated vertiginously before me, leaving an enormous absence, as though a thousand recognizable cries had occupied that space.

I remained immobile, with my eyes open, for two seconds. And suddenly, compulsively, I held myself to him, free of that horrid solitude at last!

The poison was brutal. Luis took the first step, holding me, towards the grave.

"Forgive me," he said pressing my head into the nook of his neck, "I love you so much that I take you with me."

"I love and die with you," I responded.

I could speak no longer. Yet I heard those footsteps, the voices from the corridor approaching to contemplate our agony, the frantic banging that echoed in the door.

"They followed me to separate us," I murmured. "Still, I'm yours."

When it ended, I realized that I had thought, not said, those words before losing consciousness.

*
* *

When I came to, I remember thinking that I would fall unless I leaned on something. I was light, so well rested that even opening my eyes felt sweet. I stood, in the same hotel room, propped against the back wall. And there, by the bed, was my desperate mother.

They had saved me, no? I looked everywhere and there, by the lamp, I found him standing, Luis, who recognized me at once and met me smiling. We walked straight towards each other, somehow avoiding the people that surrounded the deathbed, and said nothing, our eyes expressed the joy of having met again.

I could see, through everything and everyone, him, transparent and visible at once. It meant we were the same, dead.

We died, despite the fear of being saved that choked me as I lost consciousness. We had lost something else, luckily... And there was my mother, desperate, screaming, shaking me. I lay on the bed. The bellboy unwrapped my lover's arms from around my neck.

Distanced from each other but with our hands still intertwined, Luis and I saw everything from a clear yet slightly cold and dispassionate perspective. We lied, undoubtedly, three steps away from ourselves, dead by suicide, surrounded by the desolation of my relatives, the hotel owner, and the comings and goings of policemen. What did it matter to us?

"My love," said Luis, "we paid a small price for happiness."

"And I," I answered, "will always love you as I did. We will never be apart again?"

"No... We tried that."

"You will visit me every night?"

While we exchanged promises, my mother's shrieks reached us. They sounded violent, with an inert sonority and no eco, as though caught within a one-meter periphery around mother.

The agitation returned us to the room. They were finally carrying out our corpses, we had been dead a while, we noticed that the articulations in Luis' hands and my own had hardened, our fingers were stiff.

Our corpses... Where was this happening? Had there ever been life, any tenderness, in those heavy bodies descending the stairs, threatening to trip those that carried them.

Us, dead? How absurd! What lived in us was stronger than life and the hope for eternal love kept it alive. Before... I could not reach the threshold, crack open the door, just to see him; now we would speak every day because he could enter my home, my boyfriend.

"When will you start visiting me?" I asked.

"Tomorrow," he answered. "Let today pass."

"Tomorrow?" I continued, anguished. "Today makes no difference. Come tonight! I want to sit alone with you in the living room!"

"I do too! At nine?"

"Yes. Until then, my love…"

We separated. I walked home slowly, happily, relieved. It was as though I was returning from our first date, knowing we would meet again that night.

※ ※ ※

At exactly nine I ran to greet my boyfriend at the front door. He entered my house!

"The living room is crowded," I said. "But they won't bother us, no?"

"No… Are you there?"

"Yes."

"Very disfigured?"

"No. Can you believe it? Come see!"

We entered the room. My temples were pale and the cartilage around my dark nostrils was tense, but my face remained nearly indistinguishable from the one Luis waited to glance at from the corner.

"You look very similar," he said.

"Yes, no?" I answered happily. And lulling each other to sleep we forgot everything.

Sometimes we woke to watch the people circulating,

out of curiosity. Once I woke and called Luis' attention.

"Look," I said, pointing. "What's happening?"

The people's distressed restlessness, lively minutes before, increased when another coffin entered the room, accompanied by people I had never seen.

"It's me," said Luis, surprised. "My sisters are coming."

"They're placing our corpses in the same casket," I noticed, "as we were when we died."

"As we were meant to be," he added. At once, his eyes fixed on his sisters' faces dug in with pain. He murmured with grave tenderness, "Poor girls."

I hung to him. At once, won over by my parents' late tribute, bloody with atonement, overcoming unknowable obstacles, they buried us together.

Burying us... Absurd! Lovers, found dead on a borrowed bed but pure of body and soul, live forever. Nothing tied us to those cold, stiff, already anonymous bodies which pain had stripped of life. And yet, despite it all, we had cared too much for them, in another life, not to gift one last memory triggering gaze to those two cadaverous ghosts of love.

"They too," said my beloved, "will be eternally together."

"But I'm with you," I murmured raising my eyes to meet his, happy.

And we forgot everything again.

*

For three months—the voice persisted—I lived, fulfilled. My boyfriend visited me twice a week. He arrived punctually at nine, not a second late on a single night, and never did he arrive not to find me at the door. My boyfriend was not as punctual when leaving me. Eleven thirty struck, sometimes midnight, before he tore his hands from mine and I, my gaze from his. He finally left. I remained, surrendered to bliss, strolling through the rooms with my cheek resting on my palm.

I thought of him to make the daytime hours pass faster. I came and went from one room to the next, disinterestedly observing my family's movements, sometimes I stopped by the dining room doorway to contemplate my mother's sullen pain break into sobs while gazing at the empty seat her youngest daughter once occupied at the table.

I lived, survived, I will say it again, for and with love. What surrounded me, while I was apart from my beloved, beyond his memory, existed in a parallel world. And though I was beside my family, among them, an invisible, transparent, abyss opened between them and me, it kept us leagues apart.

We went out at night, Luis and I, an official couple. There is no walk we did not take or dusk that did not set over our idyll. When the moon was full and the temperature was sweet, we walked further, reached the outskirts, felt freer, purer, there, like lovers.

On one of those nights, our footsteps brought the

cemetery into sight, we visited the site where we lied buried underground. We entered the vast enclosed space and stopped before a somber patch of dirt from which a shiny marble headstone protruded. Nothing but our names and the date of our death burnished on its surface.

"It couldn't be a briefer memory of us," Luis observed, paused, and continued, "but it encloses more tears and regret than longer epithets." He said it, we were quiet.

Those that were there then may have witnessed two phantom fires. My boyfriend and I knew the truth, only the two specters of a double suicide enclosed under our feet were foolishly unredeemable, and another reality, life purified of error had risen with us like the two flames of one love.

We left, knowing ourselves free of memories, to saunter our bliss down the white cloudless road.

They arrived, regardless. Isolated from the world and its misconceptions, with no other purpose or thought than meeting only to meet again, our love ascended, not a supernatural force but that of the passion that would have enveloped us had we dated in another life. We sensed a sweet melancholia when together and a pure grief when apart.

I forgot to mention, my boyfriend and I hardly ever spoke when he visited, it was as though our affectionate phrases stopped expressing how we felt. He left later, while everyone slept, but our goodbyes grew shorter every night.

We left and returned in silence because I knew that

what he could say did not match what he thought, and he knew that I would say anything to avoid looking at him.

One night our unease reached the insuppressible limit of anguish. Luis bid me farewell even later than usual. He reached his hands out and I surrendering mine, cold, to him. What occurred between us was written in an intolerably clear script across his eyes. I grew as pale as death. And because his hands refused to release mine, I murmured, bewildered, "Luis!"

My incorporeal life sought desperately to lean on something, another reality. I knew he understood the horror of our situation because he let go of me and, summoning a strength I now value, his eyes recovered the expression of tenderness.

"Until tomorrow, my love," he said smiling.

"Until tomorrow, love…" I murmured, turning pale because I would never pronounce those words, again.

Luis returned the next night. We went out together and spoke, as we never had before, as we did the following nights. Everything in vain: we could no longer look at each other. We said goodbye quickly, without holding hands, a meter apart. We preferred it that way…

On the last night, my boyfriend fell at my feet and rested his head on my knees.

"My love," he started.

"Be quiet," I interrupted.

"My love," he started again.

"Keep quiet!" I retaliated, terrified, "if you say it again..."

He raised his head and our phantom eyes met—ad-mitting this is breaking my heart—for the first time in several days.

"What?" asked Luis. "What'll happen if I repeat myself?"

"You know."

"No, tell me."

"You know that I'll die!"

Our eyes remained intractably fixed on each other for fifteen seconds. In that lapse of time, destiny wove a string of infinite love stories between us, stories of desertion, reunion, rejection, resuscitation, failure and a kind of sinking into the dread of the impossible.

I turned away and murmured in response to his gaze, "I'm dying..."

Luis buried his forehead into my knees again, he also understood it all. After a while, he raised his head and spoke:

"Only one thing left for us to do..."

"Yes."

"You understand?" he insisted.

"Yes, I understand you." I laid my palms on his head and pushed to rise to standing. We started towards the cemetery, without looking at each other, again.

Oh. Do not play with love, pretend to be husband and wife, if suicide burnt the mouth you could have kissed. Do not play with life, enact a sobbing passion, if the two specters buried in a single coffin below ask you to justify the parody, the deceit. Love! The unpronounceable word exchanged for a cup of cyanide and the pleasure death brings. Oh. Ideal substance, sensation of bliss, and then, a memory or something you cry over, all your lips possess, and your arms embrace is an illusion, of love.

* * *

This kiss will cost us our lives—the voice concluded—we know. When you died of love, you must die again. Earlier, when Luis met me, I would have exchanged my soul for a kiss. He will kiss me soon, the sublime and unsustainable fog of fiction that envelops us will descend and vanish with the substantiality of touch between our always faithful mortal remains.

I ignore what awaits us there. If our love once allowed us to rise us above our poisoned bodies and live in an idyllic hallucination for three months, perhaps they, primitive and essential urns of this love, resisting the vulgarity of these contingencies, await us there.

Standing atop the gravestone, Luis and I study each other freely for a long time. His arms tighten around my waist, his mouth seeks mine, and I surrender it with such passion that I fade...

The Vampire

These are my last sentences. I just surprised the doctors sharing meaningful glances about my condition: the extreme nervous depression in which I lie ends with me.

I suffered a strong shock followed by brain fever a month ago. Still badly mended, I relapsed and was taken straight to this hospital.

Living caskets is what veterans with nervous illnesses call these isolated countryside establishments where one lies motionless in the shadows, shielded from the slightest noise. A sudden gunshot in the corridor would kill half the patients. Ceaseless grenade explosions turned these soldiers into what they are. They are laid out on their beds, dumb, inert, truly dead in the silence that cushions their frayed nervous system like dense cotton. But the slightest sudden noise—a door closing, a spoon tumbling—tears a horrible scream from them.

Such is their nervous system. They were bold and fiery assailants of war. Now, the breaking of a plate would kill them.

Though I was not in the war, I also cannot endure an unexpected noise. Just opening a shutter to let light in tears a scream from me.

But this repression of tortures does not calm my ills.

In the sepulchral twilight and limitless silence of the vast hall, I lie motionless, eyes closed, dead. But within, all my being is waylaying. My whole being, my collapse, and my agony are a white and weary anguish until death, which will overtake me soon. Moment after moment, I expect to hear beyond silence, shredded and dotted by vertiginous distance, a remote crackling.

I soon expect to see the white, concentrated, and minute ghost of a woman in the cloud over my eyes.

In a recent and immemorial past, that ghost wandered through the dining room, stopped, and then, resumed its path, unaware of its fate. After...

*
* *

I was a sturdy man with a sunny disposition and healthy nerves. One day I received a letter from a stranger asking me to expound remarks I once made about N1 rays.

Though the request was ordinary, it perplexed me that such an evidently cultured individual, as the anonymous solicitor revealed himself to be in only a few sentences, was interested in a digestible article for the general public.

I barely remembered my own article. I answered, nevertheless, with the name of the newspaper they appeared in and the approximate publication date. After doing so, I forgot the incident.

A month later, I received another letter from the same

person. He asked if I conducted the experiment mentioned in my article (he had evidently already read it) or if it was only a figment of my imagination.

I was slightly intrigued by my stranger's persistence in asking me, a mere dilettante of the sciences, what he could obtain with sacred authority from serious studies on the subject; it was evident that other sources informed my remarks on the strange performance of N1 rays. And despite this, which my cultured correspondent could not ignore, he strove for proof, from my lips, of the veracity and precision of certain optical phenomena any man of science could confirm.

I barely remembered, as I said, what I wrote about the rays in question. With effort I found, in the deepest recesses of my memory, the experience he referenced, and answered that I could guarantee that sensitive bricks put to sleep with chloroform lose their ability to emit N1 rays. Gustave Le Bon, among others, verified the phenomenon.

I answered in this tenor and forgot the N1 rays again.

Brief oblivion. A third letter arrived, with a template thank-you for my report and the following final lines, exactly transcribed, "I did not request your impressions of *that* experience. But as continuing to correspond this way will inevitably irritate you, I beg you to grant me a brief conversation in your home or wherever you wish to receive me."

Those were his words. Of course, I had discarded the initial impression that I was dealing with a mad man. Back then, I think, I already suspected what my anonymous pen pal expected from me, why he asked for my impression, what he was getting at. It was not my meager scientific knowledge that interested him.

And I finally saw this, as clearly as a man sees his image in a mirror, attentively watching him, the next day, when Guillén de Orzúa y Rosales—as he called himself—sat opposite my desk and began speaking.

I will describe his physique first. He was a man with a new lease on life, whose poise, figure, and restrained speech clearly betrayed an old and intelligently enjoyed fortune. What one first noticed about him were the habits of wealth—of the vieux riche.

The warm tone of the skin around his eyes struck me, like that of people who study cathode rays. He combed his very dark hair with an exact side part, and his tranquil, almost cold, gaze expressed the same self-assuredness and restraint as his calm poise.

Following the initial exchange:

"Are you Spanish?" I asked, taken aback that a man with his last name lacked a peninsular, or even Hispanic, accent.

"No," he answered swiftly. And, after a short pause, shared the reason for his visit:

"Though not a man of science," he said, clasping his hands on the table, "I experimented with the phenomena I alluded to in my correspondence. My fortune affords me the luxury of having a laboratory that unfortunately far surpasses my capacity to use it. I haven't discovered any new phenomena nor do I pretend to be more than a simple dilettante, devoted to mystery. I know a bit about the singular physiology—let's call it that—of N1 rays, yet, were it not, firstly, for a friend heralding your article and then, for the article itself, my ill-rested curiosity for N1 rays would not have been reawakened. Your published article concludes by suggesting a parallel between certain sound waves and visual emanations. In the same way the voice is printed in the radio circuit, the outpour of a figure can be printed in another circuit of the visual kind. If I understood (no electric energy is involved), I beg you to answer this question: Had you undergone an experience of this kind when you wrote your article or was the suggestion of corporeality just an imagined speculation? This intention and curiosity, Mr. Grant, led me to write to you twice, and then, brought me to your home, perhaps inconveniencing you."

After speaking, hands still clasped, he waited.

I answered immediately. But with the speed at which one analyzes and breaks apart a long memory before answering, I remembered the visitor's suggestion: if the retina impressed by the burning contemplation of a portrait can influence a sensitive plaque to "double" that portrait, in the same way the living forces of the soul can, when excited by those emotional rays, not produce, but "create" an image in a visual and tangible circuit...

That was the thesis argued in my article.

"I don't know," I answered immediately, "if such experiments have been carried out... That was all nothing but imaginary speculation, as you put it. My thesis shouldn't be taken seriously."

"So, you don't believe in it?"

And with his always calm, clasped hands, my visitor looked at me.

That look—which just reached me—was what pre-illuminated his true intentions for wanting to know my "personal impression."

But I did not answer.

"It isn't a mystery for me or you," he continued, "that NI rays cannot imprint anything but portraits upon sensitive bricks. Another aspect of the problem leads me to take up your precious time..."

"To ask me a question, conceding an answer?" I interrupted, smiling. "Perfect! And do you believe in it, Mr. Rosales?

"You know that I do," he responded.

If between the gaze of a stranger that shows his cards and that of another that conceals them there existed the certainty of holding the same hand, those were the circumstances in which my interlocutor and I found ourselves.

Only one stimulant of strange forces, capable of ejecting the soul in an explosion, exists: that stimulant is the imagination. NI rays did not interest my visitor at all. He ran to my home, instead, after the imaginative tangent my article pursued.

"So, you believe," I observed, "in infra-photographic impressions? You suppose I'm...a subject?"

"I'm sure," he answered.

"Have you tested it on yourself?"

"Not yet, but I will. I came to see you because I'm sure you couldn't have felt that dark suggestion, without possessing the potential to harness the rays."

"But suggestions and conjectures abound," I observed. "Asylums are full of them."

"No. They're full of 'abnormal' occurrences, not perceived 'normally,' like yours. Someone said that only what cannot be conceived is impossible. There's an unmistakable way of saying a truth that renders it recognizably true. You possess that gift."

"I have a sick little imagination..." I argued, beating a retreat.

"Mine is sick, too," he smiled. "But it's time," he added while rising to stand, "to stop distracting you. I'll end my visit with these few words: Would you like to study what we call your thesis with me? Do you feel you have the strengths to run the risk?"

"Of failure?" I inquired.

"No. We shouldn't fear failure."

"What?"

"On the contrary..."

"I believe that," I agreed. And after a pause, "Do you trust your nervous system, Mr. Rosales?"

"Very much," he turned to me, smiling with habitual calm. "It would be a pleasure to have you over when I finish my experiments. Will you allow me to see you again another day? I live alone, I have few friends, and the knowledge I have gained from you is too rich not to desire to count you as one of them."

"I'm charmed, Mr. Rosales," I bowed.

And a moment later, that strange gentleman left my company.

*
* *

Doubtlessly very strange. This cultured man, with a great fortune, without a homeland or friends, entertaining experiments stranger than being itself, awakened my curiosity. He could be a maniac, paranoid, or borderline; but it is undoubtable that he possessed great willpower… And for those that inhabit the borderland of the rational beyond, the will is the only "open sesame" for the doors to the eternally banned.

Imprisoning oneself in twilight with a sensitive plaque before one's eyes until the features of a beloved woman are imprinted on it is not a life-threatening experiment. Rosales could try it, carry it out, without any freed genies reclaiming his soul. But the inescapable and fatal slope those fantasies drag one down was what unsettled me in him and I feared in myself.

*
* *

Despite his promises, I heard nothing from Rosales for some time. One afternoon, coincidence set us side by side in the central aisle of a cinema, as we both exited during an intermission. Rosales left slowly, head held high towards the rays of light and shadow that came from the projector and traversed the room obliquely.

He seemed distracted by it, as I had to call him twice before he heard me.

"You please me so," he said. "Can you spare some time, Mr. Grant?"

"Very little," I answered.

"Perfect. Ten minutes, okay? Then, let's go somewhere, anywhere."

Once we were sitting before aligned cups of coffee that steamed sterilely:

"What's new, Mr. Rosales?" I asked. "Any results?"

"Nothing more than an impression on a sensitive plaque. It's a meager experiment I won't repeat, either. There may be more interesting things nearby… When you surprised me a moment ago, I was following the luminous beam that traversed the room. Does the cinema interest you, Mr. Grant?"

"Very much."

"I was sure. Do you believe those projection rays shaken by the life of a man carry nothing but an icy electric amplification to the screen? And forgive my effusive language… I haven't slept for days; I nearly lost the ability to sleep. I drink coffee all night, but don't sleep… And I'll proceed, Mr. Grant: Do you know what life in a painting is, and how bad paintings differ from each other? Poe's oval portrait was alive because it was painted with 'life itself.' Do you believe there can only be a galvanic imitation of life in the countenance of a woman that awakes, rises, and inflames the whole theater? Do you believe a simple photographic illusion is so capable of deceiving a man's profound understanding of feminine reality?"

And he fell silent, awaiting my answer.

Most ask questions disinterestedly. But Rosales did not ask in vain. He seriously awaited a response.

But how to respond to a man that asks this question with the accustomed measured and polite tone? Nevertheless, a moment later, I answered, "I believe you're right, half right… There's without a doubt, something other than galvanic light in a film; but it isn't life. Specters also exist."

"I never heard someone claim," he objected, "that one thousand motionless men in the dark desire a specter."

There was a long silence that I broke by standing up.

"It's been ten minutes, Mr. Rosales," I smiled.

So did he.

"You've been very kind to listen to me, Mr. Grant. Would you extend your kindness to accepting an invitation to share a meal with me next Tuesday? We'll dine alone in my home. I have an excellent cook, but he's sick... Half my staff might also be absent. But unless you're very demanding, which I don't expect, we'll make do, Mr. Grant."

"Certainly. You'll expect me?"

"If you wish."

"Delightedly. Until Tuesday, Mr. Rosales."

"Until then, Mr. Grant."

**

I had the notion that the dinner invitation had not been mere chance, nor was the cook absent due to illness, nor would I find any staff member in his home. I was wrong, nevertheless, because when I knocked on the door, I was received and handed from one member of his staff to another, until I reached the antechamber, where, after a long wait, someone apologized on behalf of the gentleman because he could not receive me: he was sick and tried to get up to excuse himself, but found it impossible. The gentleman would come to see me as soon as he could stand.

Behind the inscrutable butler and through the halfopen door, the rug in the bedroom was visible, strongly illuminated. Not a single voice was audible in the house. One could swear that vigils for the sick were held in that mute palace for months. And I had laughed with the master three days ago.

I received the following note from Rosales the next day:

"Misfortune, gentleman and friend, wanted to deprive me of the pleasure of your visit when you honored my home yesterday. Do you remember what I said about my staff? Well, this time I was ill. Don't be apprehensive: I'm well today and I'll be well next Tuesday. Will you come? I owe you compensation. I am yours, attentively, etcetera."

Again, the subject of servants. With his letter in hand, I considered with what certainty I could expect a meal in the dining room of a man whose staff was out sick or, alternatively, incomplete, and whose mansion did not offer any sign of life except a section of strongly illuminated carpet.

I once misjudged my unique friend, and was now recognizing another error. There was in his whole being and environment too much reticence, silence, and stench of crime, to take him seriously. Despite how sure Rosales was of his mental fortitude, it was evident to me that he was stumbling on the threshold of madness. Congratulating myself again for my reluctance to disturb strange forces with a man that was not Spanish but dared to use noble turns of phrase, I set out the following Tuesday to the palace of the convalescent, more predisposed to mock what I heard than enjoy my host's equivocal dinner.

But the dinner existed, though the staff did not, even the doorman that led me through the house to the dining room door, which he struck with his knuckles, vanished immediately.

A moment later the master himself half-opened the door and upon recognizing me stepped aside with a calm smile.

The first thing that caught my attention upon entering was the intensity of the warm tone, as if tanned by the sun or ultra-violet rays, which habitually tinted my friend's cheeks and forehead. He wore a tuxedo. Second, I noticed the size of the luxurious dining room, so big that the table, though placed in the third anterior of the room, seemed to be at the back. Delicacies covered the table, but there were only three place settings. At the opposite head of the table, I saw the silhouette of a woman in evening dress.

I was not, thus, the only guest. We moved into the dining room, and the strong first impression that the female silhouette awoke in me, was replaced with an acute tension when I distinguished her clearly.

She was not a woman, she was a ghost; the smiling, low-cut, and translucid specter of a woman.

I stopped for a moment; Rosales' attitude was imbued with such parti pris of being before something ordinary and common, that I proceeded alongside him. Pale and cringing, I was introduced.

"I think you already know Mr. Guillermo Grant, madam," he said to the lady, who smiled in my honor; and Rosales turned to me.

"Perfectly," I answered, bowing, as pale as a corpse.

"So, take a seat," the master said, "and deign to serve yourself whatever you like. Now you see why I had to warn you of the deficiencies in service. A poor table, Mr. Grant.... But your kindness and the presence of this lady will settle the debt."

As I said, delicacies covered the table.

Under other circumstances, the drizzle of horror would have bristled my hair and seeped into my bones. But before the parti pris of normal life, I slid into the hazy stupor that appeared to float over everything.

"And you, madam won't you serve yourself?" I turned towards the lady, after noticing that her plate was intact.

"Oh no, sir!" she answered with a tone that excuses a lack of appetite. And holding her hands against her cheek, smiled thoughtfully.

"Do you always go to the cinema, Mr. Grant?" Rosales asked me.

"Very often," I answered.

"I would've recognized you right away," the lady turned to me. "I've seen you often..."

"Very few of your films have reached us," I observed.

"But you've seen them all, Mr. Grant," the master smiled. "This explains why the lady spotted you more than once in the audience."

"Indeed," I agreed. And after an extremely long pause: "Can you distinguish the faces well from the screen?"

"Perfectly," she clarified. And added, a bit confused, "Why wouldn't I?"

"Indeed," I repeated, but this time to myself.

If I was sure I did not die on the path to Rosales' home, I had to entirely accept the trivial and mundane reality of a woman whose insides consisted only of a dress and a blurry seat backing.

We passed the time conversing about these shallow topics.

As the lady frequently raised her hand to her eyes, the master asked, "Are you tired, madam? Would you like to lie down for a few minutes? Mr. Grant and I will try to fill, with smoke, the time you leave empty."

"Yes, I'm a bit tired...," our guest agreed, standing up. "Since you excuse me," she added, smiling to one and then the other. And left, dragging her beautiful evening dress through the vitrines, whose crystals were barely veiled as she proceeded.

Rosales and I were left alone, in silence.

"What do you think of this?" he asked me after a while.

"I think," I answered, "that though I've misjudged you twice, my first impression was correct."

"You've judged me mad twice, right?"

"It isn't hard to guess..."

We were quiet for another minute. Rosales' habitual courtesy was not altered in the slightest and even less so, his characteristic discretion and restraint.

"You have a terribly strong will," I murmured.

"Yes," he smiled. "How can I hide it? I was sure of my perception when you found me in the cinema. It was 'her,' precisely. The great quantity of life betrayed by her expression revealed the potential of this phenomenon. A movie still is the impression of an instant of life, and everyone knows this. But from the moment the tape begins to run under the excitement of light, voltage, NI rays, all of her transforms into a vibrant stroke of life, more alive than fugitive life and the most vivid memories that guide our earthly race to death. But only you and I know this.

"I must confess," Rosales continued in a slightly slow tone, "that I encountered some difficulties at first. Due to a digression of the imagination, possibly, I corporified something nameless... of the kind that should remain forever on the opposite side of the tomb. It came to me and didn't abandon me for three days. The only thing *that* couldn't do was climb into bed... When you came over a week ago, I hadn't *seen* it for two hours, so I ordered that they let you in. But upon hearing your footsteps, I *saw it* tensed up by the side of the bed, trying to climb up... No, it's not something known in this world... It was an aberration of the imagination. It won't return. The next day I staked my life by ripping our guest tonight from a film... And I saved her. If someday you decide to corporify the wrong life from the screen, be careful, Mr. Grant... Beyond and behind this very moment, is Death... Release your imagination, incite it to its depths... But keep it tightly leashed, heading in the same direction at all costs, without allowing it to stray... This is a task for the will. Ignoring this has cost many existences... Allow me a vulgar simile? In a hunting rifle, the imagination is the projectile and the will, sight. Aim well, Mr. Grant! And now, let's go see our friend, who must be recovering from her fatigue. Allow me to guide you."

The thick curtaining that transposed the lady opened onto a drawing room, as vast as the dining room. A three-rung ladder led up to a platform arranged as a bedroom. In the middle stood a divan as wide as a coffin and as tall as a tumulus. On the divan, under numerous downlights arranged into a rhombus, rested the specter of a beautiful woman.

Though the carpet muffled our steps, she heard us climb the rungs. And turning to face us, with a smile still relishing in languor, she said, "I fell asleep. Forgive me, Mr. Grant, and you too, Mr. Rosales. This tranquility is so sweet..."

"Don't sit up, madam, I beg you!" the master exclaimed, recognizing her intention. "Mr. Grant and I will move two armchairs by your bedside, and we'll be able to speak comfortably."

"Oh, thank you!" she murmured. "I feel so comfortable like this!..."

Once we did what the master instructed, he proceeded,

"Now you can dawdle with Impunity, madam. Nothing urges us, nor does anything unsettle our hours. Don't you believe so, Mr. Grant?"

"Certainly," I agreed, with the same unawareness of time and the same stupor as if someone announced that I died fourteen years ago.

"I feel very well like this," replied the specter, with a hand on each temple.

And I suppose we conversed about pleasant and lively subjects, because when I left and the door closed behind me, the sun had been lighting up the streets for several long hours.

* * *

I got home and bathed right away to go out, again; but upon sitting on my bed I collapsed from exhaustion and slept for twelve hours straight. I bathed again and went out this time. My last memories floated, looming ambulatorily, unable to recall place or time. I could have fixed them, confronted each one; but all I wanted was to eat in a cheerful, noisy, and distressing restaurant, as in addition to a great appetite, I felt terrified of restraint, silence, and analysis.

I headed to a restaurant. And the door I knocked on led to Rosales' dining room, where I sat before my place setting.

Continually for a month I faithfully attended dinner there; my will did not intervene at all. During daylight hours I am sure an individual called Guillermo Grant actively pursued the habitual course of his life, with routine chores and setbacks. After nine, night after night, I found myself in Rosales' palace, first in the staff-less dining room and then in the drawing room.

Like the dreamer of Armageddon, my life under the rays of the sun has been a hallucination, and I, a ghost born to perform that role. My true existence has slipped, it was contained in a crypt, in the sweet bedroom, under the canopy of pale downlights, where, in the company of another man, we worshiped the rhombus-shaped drawings on the wall, the lights rendered homage to the specter of a woman for every heart.

For any noble heart…

"I'm not completely sincere with you," Rosales interrupted one night, meanwhile our friend, cross-legged and resting an elbow on her knee, was consumed by thought. "I wouldn't be sincere if I came across as completely satisfied with my work. I've undergone great risks to join my fate to this pure and faithful partner; and I'd give up the years I have left to bring her to life for a single moment… Mr. Grant: I've committed an inexcusable crime. Do you believe that?

"I do," I responded. "All her pain won't redeem a single errant moan from that young woman."

"I know that well… And have no right to defend what I did…"

"Undo it."

Rosales shook his head, "No, nothing could remedy…"

He paused. Then, raising his gaze and keeping the calm expression and placid tone that seemed to take him a thousand miles from the topic, he said, "I don't want reticence between us. Our friend won't emerge from the painful fog she drags herself through… without divine intervention. Only a light tap of fate can grant her the life every creation, except a monster, is entitled to."

"What light tap?" I asked.

"*Her death*, there, in Hollywood."

Rosales finished his cup of coffee and I sugared mine. Sixty seconds passed.

I broke the silence, "That won't remedy anything either…"

"You believe that?" Rosales asked.

"I'm sure… I can't tell you why, but that's how I feel. And you're not capable of doing that…"

"I'm capable, Mr. Grant. For me, for you, this spectral creation is superior to any creature living under the sun by the routine force of subsisting. Our friend is a creation of consciousness. Are you following, Mr. Grant? She answers to a nearly divine purpose; if thwarted, she'll condemn me to the tumultuous divinities who forbid all pagan gods. Will you visit occasionally during my absence? The table will be set by nightfall, as you know, and everyone leaves the house after that, except the doorman. You'll come?"

"I'll come," I answered.

"That's more than I could ask for," Rosales concluded, leaning in.

* * *

I went. If I was ever there for dinner, on most nights I arrived late, but at the same time, as punctual as a man visiting his girlfriend. At the table, the young woman and I spoke animatedly about various topics, but in the drawing room, we exchanged a few words and then fell silent immediately, won over by the stupor that flowed from the luminous cornices, and that filtered through the open door or keyhole, impregnating the palace with a morose mutism.

Coursing through the nights, our brief phrases, took the form of monotonous observations, always about the same topic, which we improvised:

"He must be in Guayaquil now," I said distractedly.

Or several nights later:

"He's left San Diego now," she said at daybreak.

One night, I, with a cigar slipping from my hand, tried to rip my gaze from the vacuum, while she, with her cheek in her hand, wandered mutely, stopped, and said, "He's in Santa Monica…"

She wandered a moment longer, and always resting her face on her hand, climbed the rungs, and laid down on the divan. I felt her without moving my eyes, since the walls of the drawing room yielded, carrying my sight, they fled fleeting into lines that converged without ever coming together. An interminable avenue of Cycas materialized in the remote perspective.

"Santa Monica," I thought, stunned.

How long went by after that, I can't remember.

Suddenly, her voice came from the divan, "He's in my house."

With the last volitional effort left in me I tore my gaze from the avenue of Cycas. Under the downlights in a rhombus entrenched in the bedroom ceiling, the young woman lied immobile, like a corpse. Before me, from a remote transoceanic perspective, the avenue of Cycas stood out diminutively with its sharply cutting line.

I closed my eyes and then saw, in a flaring vision, a man that raised a fist to a sleeping woman.

"Rosales!" I murmured, terrified. A new, gleaming flash and the murdering fist sank.

I know no more. I managed to hear a horrible cry—possibly my own—and lost consciousness.

*
* *

When I came to, I was at home, in bed. I had spent three days unconscious, hostage to a brain fever that persisted for over a month. I recovered my strength little by little. I was told a man carried me home in the small hours, I had fainted.

I remembered nothing, nor wanted to remember. I felt an extreme lassitude for thinking about anything. Later I was allowed to take brief walks around the house, which I wandered through with an absent gaze. I was finally allowed to go outside, I took some steps on the street without cognizance of my actions, without memories, without an objective… And when, in a silent room, I saw a man with a familiar face approaching, the memory and consciousness I had lost suddenly warmed my blood.

"I finally get to see you, Mr. Grant," he said, effusively shaking my hand. "Since I returned I followed the course of your illness concernedly and never doubted, not for a moment, that you'd triumph."

Rosales had lost weight. He spoke softly, as if afraid of being overheard. Over his shoulder I saw the lit bedroom and the divan I knew well, which now resembled a coffin, surrounded by tall cushions.

"Is she there," I asked.

Rosales followed my gaze and turned his eyes towards mine, calmly.

"Yes," he answered. Adding, after a brief pause, "Come."

We climbed the ladder and I leaned on the cushions.

There was nothing but a skeleton there.

I felt Rosales' hand firmly clasping my arm. And with his always stiff voice, "It's her, Mr. Grant. I feel no weight on my conscience, nor do I believe I made a mistake. When I returned from my trip, she was gone... Mr. Grant, do you remember seeing her as you passed out?"

"I don't remember..." I murmured.

"I thought so... As I did what I did on the night of your blackout, she disappeared here... When I returned, I tortured my imagination to bring her back again, from the beyond... And this is what I got! While she belonged to this world, I could corporify her spectral life as a sweet creature. I ripped life from the other to animate her ghost and she, by her complete substantiation, places a skeleton in my hands..."

Rosales stopped. I surprised his absent expression again while speaking.

"Rosales..." I began.

"Pst!" he interrupted me, lowering his tone even more. "I beg you not to raise your voice... She's there."

"She..."

"There, in the dining room . . . Oh, I haven't seen her!... But she wanders from one place to another since returning... And I feel her dress brush against me. Pay attention for a moment... Do you hear her?"

In the mute palace, through the atmosphere and immobile lights, I heard nothing. We spent a while in the most complete silence.

"It's her," Rosales murmured, satisfied. "Now listen: she dodges the chairs as she walks..."

Every night for a month, Rosales and I held a wake for the specter of bones and white lime of the one that was once our honored guest. Behind those thick curtains, which open to the dining room, the lights are still on. We know she wanders around there, numb and invisible, hurting and uncertain. In the wee hours, when Rosales and I go drink coffee, perhaps she has been occupying her seat for hours, she fixes her invisible gaze on us.

Nights succeed each other, all the same. In the atmosphere of stupor that hangs over the room, time itself seems suspended as if before an eternity. There has always been and will be a skeleton under the downlights, two friends in tuxedos in the drawing room, and a hallucination confined between the chairs in the dining room.

One night I found the atmosphere changed. My friend's excitement was visible.

"I finally found what I was seeking, Mr. Grant," he said. "I once told you I was certain I hadn't made any mistakes. Do you remember? Well, I now know I made one. You complimented my imagination, no sharper than yours, and my will, far superior. I created a visible creature with those two forces, which we lost, and a specter of bones, which will persist until... Do you know what my creation lacked, Mr. Grant?"

"A finality," I murmured, "you believed divine…"

"You said it. I began from the excitement for a moving hallucination in a dark room. I saw something more than deceit in the deep throb of passion that stirs in men before a broad and frozen photograph. Males cannot be mistaken to that point, I warned you. There must be more life there than what a ray of light and a metal curtain can simulate. That there was, you've seen. But I created it sterilely, and that was the mistake I made. What the happiness of the deepest spectator would create, didn't find enough heat in my cold hands and fainted… Love isn't necessary in life, but it is indispensable before death's door. If I'd killed for love, today my creature would pulsate with life on the divan. I killed to create, lovelessly; and obtained life at its brutal root: a skeleton. Mr. Grant: Will you leave me for three days and return next Tuesday to dine with us?"

"With her?…"

"Yes; you, her, and me… Have no doubt… Next Tuesday."

*
* *

As I let myself in, I saw her again, in fact, dressed in her habitual magnificence, and I confess that it was very gratifying to recognize her trust in seeing me. She shook my hand and smiled, an open smile for a faithful friend upon returning from a long journey.

"We've missed you very much, madam," I said effusively.

"So have I, Mr. Grant!" she answered, resting her head on her clasped hands.

"You missed me? Really?"

"You? Oh, yes, very much!" and turned to smile at me for some time.

At that moment I realized that the master had not raised his gaze from his fork since we started talking. Was it possible?...

"And our host, madam: Did you miss him?"

"Him?..." She murmured slowly. And sliding her hand from her cheek without haste, she turned to face Rosales.

Then, I saw the most ridiculous flame of passion a woman has ever felt for any man flicker across her eyes, fixed on him. Rosales also saw it. And the man grew pale before that vertiginously unreserved expression of feminine love.

"Him too..." The young woman murmured with a gentle and exhausted voice.

Over the course of the meal, she affected indifference for the master while chatting copiously with me, and he barely abandoned his game with the fork. But the two or three times their gazes met as if by accident, I saw the uncontainable heat of desire flash across her eyes and settle immediately, fainting.

And she was a specter.

"Rosales!" I exclaimed when we had a moment alone.

"If you have any love for life left, destroy that! It'll kill you!"

"Her? Are you mad, Mr. Grant?"

"Not her, her love! You can't see it because you're under her dominion. I see it. No man can resist the passion of that... ghost."

"I repeat that you're wrong, Mr. Grant."

"No, you just can't see it! Your life has resisted several trials, but it'll burn like a feather, if you continue exciting that creature."

"I don't desire her, Mr. Grant."

"But she does desire you. She's a vampire and you have nothing to surrender to her! Do you understand?"

Rosales responded with nothing.

The girl's voice came from the drawing room, or the beyond, "Will I be alone much longer?"

At that moment, I suddenly remembered the skeleton that lay there...

"The skeleton, Rosales!" I clamored, "What happened to her skeleton?"

"It returned," he answered. "It returned to the void. But she is there now, on the divan... Listen to me, Mr. Grant: no creature has ever forced itself on its creator... I created a ghost; and, mistakenly, a sack of bones. You're ignorant of some details of the creation process... Hear them now. I acquired a flashlight and projected the reels that feature our friend on a screen sensitive to N_1 rays. (Do you remember the N_1 rays?) Using a vulgar instrument, I kept in motion photographic instants in which the woman that watches us seemed most alive... You know well that in all of us, as we speak, there are moments of such conviction, of such timely inspiration, that we notice in the gazes of others and feel in ourselves a part of us projecting forward... She released herself from the screen that way, flowing mere millimeters from it initially, and finally came to me, just as you've seen her... That was three days ago. She is there..."

The woman's languid voice reached us from the bedroom again, "Are you coming, Mr. Rosales?"

"Undo this, Rosales," I exclaimed, grabbing his arm, "before it's too late! Don't excite that monster with more feeling."

"Goodnight, Mr. Grant," he sent me away with a smile, leaning in.

*
* *

And so, this story ends. Did Mr. Rosales find strength in this world to resist? I'll find out very soon—perhaps today.

I was not surprised when I received an urgent telephone call that morning, nor when I saw the curtains of the room gilded by the fire, the projector on the floor, and remnants of burnt films scattered on the floor. Stretched out on the rug, by the divan, Rosales' dead body.

The staff claimed that the projector was transported to

that room on previous nights. They are under the impression that due to an oversight, the films caught on fire, the sparks of which reached the cushions on the divan. The death of the gentleman was attributed to a cardiac lesion, precipitated by the accident.

I am under another impression. The calm expression on his face was unaltered and, even in death, his countenance conserved its habitually warm tone. But I am certain not a drop of blood remained in the deepest innards of his veins.

The Flies

While razing the forest, the men fell this tree last year, the entire extent of its trunk lies crushed against the ground. Its companions have lost most of their bark to the clearing fire but that one's is nearly intact. Nearly, the carbonized band along its length clearly speaks to the action of the fire.

That occurred last winter. Four months have passed. Midst the clearing lost to the draught, the fallen tree, forever in a wasteland of ashes. Leaning against the trunk, my back resting on it, I find myself also immobile. At a point along my back the vertebral column is broken. I fell precisely there, after lucklessly stumbling on a root. As I fell, I remain, seated—better said, broken—against the tree.

An instant ago I started sensing a fixed hum—the hum of the spinal cord lesion—that floods everything, and into which my breath seems to course and dissolve. I can no longer move my hands, barely stir the ashes with one finger or another.

From that same instant I acquire the clear and capital certainty that my life grazing earth awaits the instantaneity of a few seconds when it will extinguish itself entirely.

This is the truth. Never has a more decisive one materialized in my mind. All the others float, dance in a distant reverberation of another *I*, in a past that does not belong to me either. My only perception of existence, as blatant as a blow delivered in silence, is that I will die an instant from now.

But, when? What are these seconds and instants during which this exasperated conscience of living still courses through a placid corpse?

No one approaches this clearing: no forest trail leads to it from any property. True for the seated man and the trunk holding him, successive rains will drench bark and clothes, and suns will dry lichen and hair, until the regrowth of the forest unites trees and potash, bones and shoe leather.

Nothing, nothing in the serene atmosphere betrays such an event, no one cries. Rather, peer between the trunks and black segments of the clearing, stand here or there, regardless of the perspective, anyone can contemplate the perfectly delineated figure of the man whose life is about to stop on the ashes, attracted like a pendulum to gravity: the place he occupies within the clearing is so small and his situation, so clear: he is dying.

This is the truth. Transcend the dark animal resistance, the beat and the breath threatened by death. What is it worth before the barbarous disquiet of the precise instant this resistance of life and tremendous psychological torture implode like a rocket, leaving a former man, his face always fixed forth, as the only residue?

The hum grows ever stronger. It now hangs over my eyes like a veil of dense fog through which green rhombuses are delineable. And immediately I see the fortified wall of a Moroccan bazaar, a herd of white studs escape through one of its double-leaf doors, while a theory of decapitated men enters through the other.

I want to close my eyes but no longer can. Now I see a small hospital room, where four doctors I know strive to convince me that I will not die. I observe them in silence and they, following my thoughts, burst into laughter.

"Well," says one, "the cage of flies is the last test to your conviction. I have one."

"Flies?"

"Yes," he responds, "green detection flies. You know that green flies sense the decomposition of meat long before the demise of the subject. They find the still live patient, sure of their prey. They hover without haste or losing sight of it, they smelled his death. It is the most effective prediction method known. That is why the sense of smell of the ones I own has been refined through selection. I rent them out at a moderate rate. Where they enter, sure prey. I can leave them in the corridor when you are left alone and open the door to their cage which, I mention in passing, is a small coffin. Your only task is to open the keyhole. If a fly enters and you hear it buzz, know the others will find a path that leads to you. I rent them out at a moderate rate."

"A hospital?" Suddenly the small white room, the first-aid kit, the doctors, and his laugh fade into a hum...

And abruptly, the revelation takes shape within me, too. The flies!

They are the ones that buzz. Since I fell, they found me without delay. The flies dozing in the forest, due to the effect and range of the fire, awoke aware of a sure proximate prey, I do not know how. They smelled the ensuing decomposition of the seated man, perceiving qualities imperceptible to us, perhaps the fractured spinal medulla exhaled through the flesh. They found me with immediacy and hover above me without haste, measuring with their eyes the proportions of the nest luck has granted their eggs.

The doctor was right. His profession could not be more lucrative.

Yet it is here that this desperate yearning to resist placates and yields to a blessed unknown. Now I no longer feel rooted by grave torture to a fixed place on earth. I feel the dense atmosphere turn light, the light of the sun, the fecundity of the hour pour out of me like life itself. Free of space and time, I can go here, there, to this tree, that vine. I can see, far now, like a memory of a remote existence, I can still see, at the foot of a trunk, a doll with eyes that don't blink, a scarecrow of glazed gaze and rigid legs. From the core of this expansion, dilated by the sun which pieces apart my conscience into a billion particles, I can pick myself up and fly, fly...

And fly, and perch beside my companions on the fallen trunk, under the rays of the sun that lend their fire to our work of vital renovation.

The Express Train Conductor

108 conductors afflicted with mental alienation were admitted into the Mercedes Asylum between 1905 and 1925.

One morning, a squalid man, with a gaunt face, that could barely hold himself up, arrived at the asylum. He was dressed in rags and articulated his words so poorly that one had to discover what he said. Regardless, as his wife affirmed with some pretension when admitting him, a few hours earlier, the conductor had steered his machine.

At some point during that timespan, a deranged signalman and switchman worked on the same line as two mentally alienated conductors.

It is time, given the copious noted facts, to meditate on the easily imaginable behaviors the deranged conductor of a train incurs.

That is what I read in the criminology, psychiatry, and medical law magazine I hold before my eyes while I have breakfast.

Perfect. I am one of those conductors. Better yet: I am the conductor of the Continental Express. Well, I read the aforementioned study with an equally imaginable attentiveness.

Men, women, children, toddlers, presidents, and lunatics: distrust psychiatrists as you would the police. They are the mental comptrollers of humanity and thus, benefit— keep your eyes open! I do not know the statistics of derangement among hospital staff; but I would not exchange a madman astride a locomotive that undergoes disorders on the tracks, for a depressed psychiatrist before an asylum.

Still beware that the specialist who the previously noted paragraphs belong to confirms the derangement of 108 conductors and 186 boilermen in the span of twenty years, in truth, establishing a little alarming proportion: over five mad conductors a year. And when I say conductors, I refer to both occupations; since, nobody ignores that a boilerman possesses sufficient technical capacity to drive his machine, in case of a chance accident.

Considering this, I only desire that this percentage of madmen guiding the fate of a portion of humanity is as weak in our profession as in theirs.

With that I calmly finish my coffee, which tastes oddly salty today.

※ ※
※

I meditated on this fifteen days ago. Today, I lost the tranquility I had then. I feel perfectly definable things, if only I was certain of what I want to define. Sometimes, when gazing into someone's eyes while I speak, I feel that my gestures and those of my interlocutor are suspended in static hardness, though actions proceed; and that an eternity rests between word and word, though we do not cease speaking quickly.

I return to myself, not nimbly, as if returning from a momentary bewilderment, but in the waves and dizzying beats of a recovering heart. I remember nothing of that state; and, regardless, retain the impression and exhaustion of enduring grave emotions.

Other times I abruptly lose the comptroller of my *I*, and from a corner in the machine, transformed into a being so small, concentrated lines as lucent as an octagonal screw, I see myself maneuvering with anguished slowness.

What is that? I do not know. I have been on this route for eighteen years. My sight remains normal. Unfortunately, one always knows more about pathologies than convenient, and I resort to the company's medical practice.

"I feel nothing in any organ," I said, "but I don't want to end up epileptic. It's inconvenient for anyone to see moving things still."

"And all that?" the doctor asked, watching me. "Who diagnosed you?"

"I read it somewhere," I responded. "I beg you, please examine me."

The doctor examined my stomach, liver, circulation, and sight, as you would expect.

"I see nothing," he said to me, "aside from the slight

depression you admit to by coming here... Think less, aside from the indispensable to maneuver, and read nothing. It does not suit an express train conductor to see double, and less so to understand why."

"But wouldn't it be prudent," I insist, "to request a complete examination from the company? I carry responsibilities too great for..."

"Let me finish your sentence:... for the brief examination I conducted. You're right, my conductor friend. It isn't only prudent but indispensable. Go calmly to your exam; conductors that confuse the levers do not reason as you have."

I shrugged when he turned his back, and left more depressed.

Why see a company doctor if every rational treatment will set me under a regime of ignorance?

When a man possesses a culture superior to his occupation, he suspects himself before his employers. If these suspensions of life continue and sight doubled or tripled by a distant transparency accentuates, then, I will know what is advisable for a train conductor in such a state.

* *

I am happy. I woke up at dawn, no longer tired and so aware of my wellbeing that my small house, the streets, the entire city seemed too small to be inhabited by my fullness of life. I went outside, singing within, with my fists clenched and a slight external smile, as all men that feel worthy before the awakening of vast creation.

It is strange how a man can suddenly turn and see that above, below, to the east, to the west there is nothing but latent clarity, whose infinitesimal ions consist of satisfaction: simple and noble satisfaction that pours from the chest and makes the head rise beatifically.

Before, in a remote time and place, I was depressed, so heavy with anguish that I could not raise myself a millimeter off the flat ground. There are gasses that drag themselves that way across the low earth unable to lift themselves off her, and trawl asphyxiating because they cannot breathe on their own.

I was one of those gasses. I can now stand alone, without help from anyone, even the highest clouds. And if I was a man that extends his hands and blesses everyone, everything and waking life would follow an illuminated path: such is the true expansive reach of a man's mind!

From this height and radial perfection, I remember the miseries and collapses that keep me on the surface of the earth, like a gas. How could this firm flesh of mine and this insolent fulfillment of contemplation, harbor such incertitude, sordidness, mania, and asphyxiation due to lack of air?

I peer around and find myself alone, safe, musical, and laughing at my harmonious existence. The life, heavy tractor and caboose at once offers these phenomena: the back wheels of a locomotive break suddenly and it finds itself illuminated by the sun! From every side! Upright and under the sun!

How little you need to decide your fate: at the height swollen, calm, and efficient, or on the surface of the earth like a gas!

I was a gas. Now I am what I am. I return home slowly and enchanted.

* *

I have coffee with my daughter on my lap, bearing an attitude that surprises my wife.

"I last saw you like this a long time ago," she says with her serious and sad voice.

"It is life reborn," I respond. "I'm another, sister!"

"I hope you'll stay as you are," she murmurs.

"When Fermín bought his house, the company said nothing to him. There was an extra key."

"What are you saying?" my wife asks, raising her head.

I look at her, more surprised by her question than she is, and respond, "What I said: I'll stay like this!"

With that I stand and walk out again.

I usually go by the office after lunch to receive orders and do not return to the station until it is time to occupy my seat. There is no novelty today, aside from the great rains. Somedays, I leave the house with an inexplicable somnolence; and others, I arrive at the machine with a strange yearning.

Today I do it all without rushing, with the watch before the brain and the things I must see, radiating from their exact centers.

In this fortunate conjunction of time and destinations, we pull out. We run half an hour behind train 248. My machine is 129. The pillars of the Perendén platform reflect on its bronze numeral at their passing pace.

I have eighteen years of service, without one infraction, punishment, or accusation. That is why the chief said to me before departing, "Two accidents this month is enough. Careful with juncture three. Once you've passed it, keep an eye on path 296 to 315. You can make up for lost time later. I warn you because I know we can trust your nerve. Good luck and inform us as soon as you arrive."

Keep your nerve! Nerve! Oh, boss! It is unnecessary to recommend calm to this soul! I can drive the train blind. The ballast is made of lines, not spots. When I put my nerve on the tip of the crinoline it scratches the ballast! Lascazes didn't have change for the cigarettes he bought on the bridge...

For some time I have been watching the boilerman shovel with an overwhelming slowness. Each of his movements seems isolated, as though constituted by some very hard material. What a partner the company entrusted me to save...

"My friend!" I scream, "And your courage? Didn't the boss recommend nerve? The train is running like a cockroach."

"Cockroach?" he responds, "We are at the limit... two pounds over. This carbon is not like the one we had last month."

"We have to run, my friend! And your nerve? I found mine."

"What?" murmured the man.

"The juncture! We have to shovel firmly when we reach it. And then, from 296 to 315."

"With this rain pounding us?" objects the timorous one.

"The boss... Keep your nerve! After eighteen years of service, I understand every meaning of that phrase. Let's run at 110, my friend!"

"If it was up to me..." Concluded the man, studying me for a while out the corner of his eye.

I understand him! Oh, the fulfillment of feeling in one's heart, like a universe made exclusively of light and fidelity, this tranquility that exalts me! A train engineer of whom nerve is demanded when dealing with a certain juncture is but a being made wretched, miniscule, and hand-tied by rules and terror! It is not the mechanic in blue, with the cap, handkerchief, and wage, who can scream at his superiors: I am the embodiment of calm! Each thing must be perceived from its isolated summit of existence! Understand it with astonished joy! One needs to possess a soul in which everyone possesses a sense. One needs to be the immediate factor of everything that craves contact to become! Be me!

Engineer. Take a look outside. The night is very black. The train is running with its ladder of reflections dragging behind and the rivets of the railcars are swollen. The once immobile banister before the boiler separates itself from the window and undulates more and more, until it sweeps the rim of the track from one side to the other.

I dip my head back in: at this very moment, the light of the open hearth radiates enveloping the sweater of the immobile boilerman. Immobilized with the shovel raised above him and the sweater bristling with lint in pale firelight.

"Wretch! You've abandoned your post!" I roar, launching myself from the sandpit.

*
* *

Spectacular tranquility. In the field, at last, outside the railway routine!

Yesterday, my dying daughter. Poor daughter of mine! Today, frankly convalescent. We are detained beside a wire fence watching the sweet morning progress. Beside each side of our daughter's stroller, that we have dragged here, my wife and I look into the distance, happy.

"Father, a train!" says my daughter pointing her slim

fingers that we kiss in duet with her mother every night.

"Yes, little one," I affirm. "It's the 7:45 express."

"It's going fast, father!" she noticed.

"Oh! There's no danger at all; it can run. But at the st..."

*
* *

Like a noiseless explosion, the atmosphere enveloping my head flees in fleeting waves, suctioning part of my brain—and I see myself again in the sandbox, driving my train.

I have done something in multiplying contact that besieges me but which I cannot remember. Little by little my attitude collects itself, my back arches, my nails bury into the lever... And I let out a long, stertorous meow!

Suddenly, with a "crack!" and livid lightning, the turmoil I started feeling weeks ago materializes, I understand I am losing my mind.

Mad! It is necessary for this sensation to strike in the fullness of life and moan with supreme aspiration, a thousand times worse than death, to understand the fully beastly shriek with which the brain howls the loosening of its screws!

Mad! That impression strikes accompanied by the shriek of a cat! I meowed! I shrieked like a cat!

"My nerve, my friend! I need to recover... Ready, chiefs!"

I throw myself on the ground again.

"Hand-tied boilerman!" I scream at him through his gag.

"My friend! You've never seen a man go mad? Watch: Prrr!"

"Because you're a man with nerve, we trust you with the train. Watch out for track gauge 4004! Cat," that is what the chief said.

"Boilerman! We'll shovel firmly and eat up gauge 29000000003!"

* * *

I let go of the key and see myself again, dark and insignificant, driving my train. The tremendous jolts of the locomotive stab my brain. We are passing juncture 3!

Then, the words of the psychiatrist appear at the tips of my eyelashes: "... the easily imaginable behaviors the deranged conductor of a train incurs.

Oh! Being deranged is nothing. What is horrible is feeling incapable of containing, not only the train, but a miserable human reason that flees with the overloaded valves at full steam! What is horrible is being conscious that this last carat of reason will vanish as well, without the tremendous responsibility that strains to contain it! I only ask for one hour! Only ten minutes! An instant from now... If only I had time to untie the boilerman and bury him.

"Quick! Help me..."

As I crouch, the lid of the sandbox lifts and a flock of rats pours into the heath.

Fucking beasts... they will extinguish the fire! I fill the

heath with carbon, I fasten the timorous one over the sandbox and sit on the other.

"My friend!" I yell at him, with one hand on the lever and the other in the eye. "One seeks accomplices to delay a train, no? What'll the boss say about his rat collection? He'll say: watch out for the mmm... millionth gauge! And who crosses it at 113 kilometers? A servant. Rat fur. That's me! I am certain of nothing but what is before me, and the company kills for people like me. 'What are you?' They ask. Discreet attitude and essential preponderance! I respond! My friend! Hear the train shake... We crossed the gauge...

Stay calm, boss! It won't jump, I say so... Jump, my friend! Now I see it! Jump...

It didn't jump! You were really frightened, mister! And why? I asked. Who is the only one that deserves his superiors' trust? Ask, stablemaden from hell, or I will bury this fire iron in your stomach!"

"Look at this train," says the station chief looking at his watch. "It won't be late. It's twelve minutes ahead."

Follow the line. See the express advance like a monster knocking from one side to the other, advancing, arriving, roaring past, and fleeing at 110 kilometers per hour.

"Does anyone know?" I say to the boss showing off with my hands on my chest. "Does anyone know this train's destination?"

"Destination?" the boss turns to the engineer, "Buenos Aires, I suppose..."

The engineer smiles shaking his head softly, winks at the station chief, and raises the tips of his restless fingers to the highest part of the atmosphere.

And I throw the fire iron to the track, drenched in sweat: the boilerman has saved himself.

But the train has not. I know that this last section will be even briefer than the others. If a moment ago I did not have time — no material: mental — to untie my assistant and hand the train over to him, I will not have the time to stop it either... I put my hand on the key to clo-o-ose. Pf, pf! My friend! Another rat!

Last radiance... What horrible martyrdom! God of reason and of my poor daughter! Concede me enough time to place my hand on the white-prrrwhite-lever! Meow!

The chief of the station that precedes the terminal just had time to hear the conductor of the 248-express, nearly falling out of the carriage door, scream in a tone he will never forget, "Divert me!"

But what descended from the train afterwards, whose grinded breaks had stopped it by the detour bumper; what was pulled out by force from the locomotive, meowing horribly and writhing like a beast, was but a rag for the rest of his days in the asylum. The psychiatrists believe that saving the train — and the 125 lives it carried — evidenced professional automatism, not very rare, and that those with this kind of illness tend to recover their judgment.

We believe that the sense of duty, profoundly rooted in the nature of man, is capable of containing for three hours the tide of madness that is drowning him. But one does not recover from such mental heroism.

The Call

Coincidence brought me that morning to the sanatorium, where the woman had been admitted four days earlier, after the catastrophe.

"It'll be worth your while," said the doctor I was visiting, "to hear the story of the accident. You'll see a rare case of obsession and auditory hallucination, unique in its presentation.

The poor woman suffered a strong shock with the death of her daughter. For the first three days she did not bat an eyelash, her open eyes expressed an indescribable anguish. Listening to her will not be a waste for any of you. I include the two gentlemen ascending the stairs in that plural *you*, they're spiritualist society delegates, or something like that. Regardless of them, remember what I said a moment ago about the patient: state of obsession, fixed idea, and auditory hallucination. Those gentlemen are here now. Let's go."

It is not difficult to provoke a poor woman, a few caring words incite mute tears that release her from the tight grip of anguish, to confide what will give vent to her heart. Covering her face with her hands, "What can I say," she murmured, "that I haven't told my doctor already..."

"We wish to hear the whole story, ma'am," the former

requested. "In its entirety and detail."

"Oh! The details..." The patient still murmured, uncovering her face and slowly nodding, "Yes, the details... I remember them one by one... And even if I live a thousand years..."

She abruptly covered her eyes with her hands and kept them there, pressing firmly, as if behind that veil she sought to finally concentrate and expel the hallucinatory tumult of memories.

A moment later the hands were falling and, with a feeble yet calm countenance, she began, "I'll do what you ask. A month ago..."

The doctor noted, softly, "From the beginning, ma'am..."

"All right, Doctor... I'll do that... You've been very kind to me... And only fifteen days ago... Yes, yes! I'm getting there, Doctor... It's what I wanted to say. One thousand... Our little girl was exactly four years and one month old when her father fell ill and never rose again. We'd never been happy. My husband was of delicate constitution and too meek to fight to live. I don't know what would've become of us if we hadn't been well-off. He always seemed to miss something, even when he smiled at us. And I don't believe he experienced happiness until he became a father.

But he had such love for his daughter, Doctor! Such religious devotion when contemplating our girl! And what consolation for me that he finally found something to tie him strongly to life!

He doubtlessly loved me when he could; but only his daughter's tiny hands dissipated his eternal sadness.

He lied down, as I said, and never rose again. My wife's pain vanished before the unnarratable pain expressed in the eyes of the father that had to separate himself from his daughter forever.

Forever, Doctor! His last look, fixed on me, revealed so intensely what his heart held, that I closed his eyes with my lips, saying, 'Sleep in peace! I'll watch over your daughter like you would've.'

We were left alone then, my little one and I; she sold health with her rosy cheeks, while I recovered beside her from my drawn-out devastation.

My little one! She seemed to take on her poor father's strength: the joy of her countenance illuminated our existence. The promise I made to my husband on his deathbed was not in vain. Like him, I now channeled the immensity of my love and solitude into our daughter.

Oh! I watched over her, believe me, as if my life and the entire world had no other fate or end than to serve my daughter's happiness. What future joys haven't I dreamt up for the little one asleep in my arms, while refusing to lay her down? How light the sacrifice of exhaustion seemed to me, if with it I could infuse her little body with what was left of my life!

Yes, extreme exhaustion... I already explained how I felt then, Doctor. I was recovering externally, I gained weight and my countenance improved; but something was dying in the depths of my hopes, draining day after day. I lost the thread of my dreams of good fortune soon after weaving them and was left inert, with my head hanging low, and mortally tired, as if an infinite and frozen emptiness extended before my illusions. Sometimes, I don't know from where, I seemed to perceive, though barely perceptible, due to the distance, a voice that pronounced my daughter's name. I was so, so tired!

I could no longer dream of the hereafter without the sadness of the void, the horrible sterility of my strength, freezing my heart. Why? No reason existed, no, none to suffer this way. My girl was there, healthier and happier every day. We didn't nor could lack anything, given our position. No, nothing! And squeezing our daughter tightly in my arms, I knew that the hereafter was all ours. That was what I swore to my husband.

The hereafter... Yet when I began to forge a dream of happiness for my girl, the daydream froze — oh, such a horrible chill — as if her father's love and my own didn't suffice to feed it. And I fell, dejected, into a profound disillusionment.

This state of anguish lasted a month. One night, as I thought for the millionth time about the endearing care that would always envelop my girl, at that very moment I heard these nitid words, *There'll be no need.*

Oh! It is very hard for a poor mother whose little girl's happiness leaves her sleepless to perceive a voice warning that her efforts to obtain it will be useless! This lugubrious voice finally justified my truncated dreams and mortal sadness. Within me, to become even more unquestionable, the voice found an echo and warned me that my daughter would have no need for…

Because she'd die!

Oh, God! Our little girl, dead, the one for whom her mother and father gave their whole lives! Oh, no, no! I rebelled, Doctor! What did a voice announcing my beloved daughter's death matter to me, if I dared to defend her against everything and everyone?

From that moment on my existence was but a terrifying nightmare, without another reason to exist than the desperate defense of my girl's life! 'I'll watch you!' I yelled at myself. And at that precise moment, from the shadowy depths of our fate, the voice intensified its warning, telling me, *Everything you do is useless.*

Then… Then, my little girl had to die… 'My God!' I clamored, breaking down sobbing on my girl's neck. Could the voice that announces a daughter's death in a mother's heart deny her the strength to avoid it?

Everything you do is useless.

Oh, no one has invented a greater torment than the one I endured! To die! But, of what? Illness? An accident?

An accident!

I was certain of it before I heard the words, *She'll die by accident.*

Oh! I'm summarizing, Doctor... We used to go out every afternoon. We stopped. I checked the solidity of the furniture ten times in a row. I banged on the walls for hours on end. I had everything that did not guarantee safe use removed from our home. I wandered from one stripped room to another, with my heart drowning in omens. I checked one and a hundred times what I examined before.

I felt emptied of everything. There was nothing but shock and terror in me, which my impulse obeyed robotically. My girl was constantly beside me, under the triple guardianship of my heart, eyes, and hands.

With each minute, nevertheless, the moment inexorably approached.

'What, my God?!' I clamored in my anguish, 'What accident should I ward her against, save her from, despite everything?'

While I smothered my girl in my arms, I suddenly had the horrible revelation: *She'll die by fire.* And immediately afterwards, the entire house, my breath, my clothes issued the terrible certainty that my daughter's days were counted: not in months or days, but brief hours...

I raced to the kitchen like a mad woman, extinguished the fire, and threw buckets of water on the ashes. I ordered that fire never be lit for any reason. I confiscated all the boxes of matches in the house and threw them in the bathroom. I still ran from room to room like a mad woman, feverishly checking the drawers of every item of furniture in the house. I closed all the doors and windows, ran back to the kitchen to check that no one disobeyed, and took refuge with my daughter in my husband's study, he fortunately never smoked.

Fire... Oh, no! We were safe there!

But instead of finding serenity, my anguish grew lacerating with every second. And if I had missed something? If the cook saved a box of matches? And if a supplier came to the kitchen and lit a cigarette...

Oh! The danger lied there! That was it! And letting my girl fall from my lap with a cry, I rushed to the service quarters... And the cook barely had time to match my screams: a detonation made the house shake..."

The poor mother fell silent. For a long time, perhaps enough to dim the last roar of the stampede in her soul, her hands still covered her eyes. Finally, "Yes... You know the rest, Doctor... I also knew it before I saw my daughter dead on the floor... Yes... During my brief absence she opened the desk drawers and took a gun that lay deep within one... The weapon fell from her hands..."

"Doctor," she exclaimed abruptly with her whole voice, revealing her desperate countenance, "I lost my daughter, you know this, as was predicted... With a coldness and cruelty only God witnessed, I was warned that my daughter would not need my care… I was warned all I did to avoid her death was useless… And finally, I was assured she'd die by fire.

By fire, sir! Why wasn't I told that a bullet or the shot of a firearm would kill her, which I could've prevented. Why trip up a mother's heart and the life of an innocent? Why was I allowed to seek matches madly, without warning the danger lied elsewhere? How could God consent to turning my pain into a simple play on words, to ripping my daughter from me more horridly? Why?…"

And her voice drowned, cut by the violence with which her hands rose to clasp her face.

A long, very long silence supervened. One of the visitors finally broke it, "Ma'am, you told us you heard a voice augur your terrible misfortune."

A deep shudder traversed the patient; but she did not answer.

"You also described," the visitor proceeded, "a deeply distant voice on several occasions. Did the same voice call to your daughter and vainly warn against danger?"

The patient nodded.

"Did you recognize that voice?"

And this time, she finally surrendered an endless sob into her pillow, the poor mother responded from the depths of her horror, "Yes, it was her father's…"

The Son

It is a powerful summer's day in Misiones, all the sun, heat, and tranquility latent in the season is aroused. Nature, exposed, feels satiated.

The father bares his heart to nature imitating the sun, heat, and tranquil atmosphere.

"Take care, little one," he condenses all the cautions the case entails in this phrase, and his son understands perfectly.

"Yes, father," responds the child grasping the rifle and loading bullets in his shirt pockets which he closes carefully.

"Return for lunch," the father still instructs.

"Yes, father," repeats the son.

He balances the rifle in his hand, smiles at his father, kisses him on the head, and departs.

The father follows him with his eyes for a while and then resumes his tasks for that day, contented by his little one's joy.

He knows that his son, educated in the habitual precaution of danger from the tenderest infancy, can handle a firearm and hunt no matter what. Though tall for his age, he is only thirteen. And seems younger, judging by the purity of his blue eyes, still fresh with infantile awe.

The father does not need to look up from his tasks to follow the son's progression with his mind. He has crossed the red footpath and heads to the forest through the clearing in the esparto grass.

To hunt in the forest—wildfowl hunt—requires more patience than his pup can yield. After traversing that forested island, his son skirts the cacti border until he reaches the swamp, in search of pigeons, toucans, or that pair of herons his friend Juan discovered a few days ago.

For now, the memory of those two boys' passion for venery sketches a smile on the father's face. They only ever catch a yacútoro or, less often, a surucúa and return triumphant. Juan, to his ranch with the nine-millimeter gun the other boy's father gave him. His son, to the plateau with his 16 caliber, white gunpowder, quadruple closure Saint-Etienne rifle.

He was like him. At thirteen he would have given his life for a rifle. His son, that age now, owns one—the father smiles.

It is still difficult for a widowed father, for whom the life of his son is his sole source of faith and hope, to educate him as he has: free in his limited-action radius, sure on his small hands and feet since he was four, and conscious of the gravity of certain dangers and the scarcity of his own strength.

That father has firmly fought against what he considers his egotism. A child can so easily make an error in judgment, set a foot in the void, and one loses a son.

The danger subsists for man at any age; but its threat slackens once accustomed since boyhood to count only on one's strength.

This is how the father educated his son. And to achieve it he has resisted his heart, but also moral torment; this father of weak stomach and sight, has been enduring hallucinations.

He has seen, materialized in painful illusions, memories of a happiness that should not resurge from the nothingness it imprisons itself in. He once saw the boy shoot the bench vise of the workshop with a parabellum bullet and roll wrapped in blood, when in fact he was only filing the buckle on his hunting belt.

A horrible incident. But today, that ardent and vigorous summer's day, the love for which his son seemingly inherited, the father feels happy, calm, and sure of the hereafter.

At that moment, not far, a shot resounds.

"The Saint-Etienne," the father identifies the source when he recognizes the explosion. Two pigeons less in the forest...

Paying no more attention to the trivial event, the man withdraws into his work.

The sun, now high, continues to ascend. Wherever you look—stones, earth, trees—the air, congested as in an oven, vibrates with heat. The deep hum fills the entire being and permeates the atmosphere as far as the eye can reach, condensing all of life in the tropics in that instant.

The father takes a look at his wrist: it is twelve. And raises his gaze to the forest.

His son should be back by now. Their mutual trust renders them — the silver-haired father and the thirteen-year-old creature — unable to deceive each other. When his son responds, "Yes, father," he obeys. He said he would return at twelve, and the father smiled watching him depart.

And he has not returned.

The man turns to his work, forcing himself to focus on the task at hand. It is so easy to lose track of time in the forest and sit on the ground for a while, resting, immobile.

Time has passed: it is twelve thirty. The father leaves his workshop. Resting his hand on the mechanic's bench, the detonation of a parabellum bullet rises from the depths of his memory. Instantly, for the first time in the three hours that have passed, he realizes that he has heard nothing after the shot of the Saint-Etienne. He has not heard the gravel rolling under a familiar pace. His son has not returned, and nature finds itself suspended at the edge of the forest, waiting for him.

Oh, tempered character and blind trust in a son's education do not suffice to spook the specter of fatality a father with ill sight sees rise from the forest line. Distraction, oblivion, and fortuitous delay: none of these trivial motives for his son's delayed return resonate with that heart.

A shot, a single shot, resounded, too long ago. After it, the father has not heard a sound, has not seen a bird, not one person has crossed the threshold announcing that upon crossing the wire fence, he witnessed a great tragedy.

The father enters with a bare head and without an axe. Cuts through the clearing in the espartillo grass, enters the forest, and skirts the border of cacti without finding the faintest trace of his son.

But nature remains suspended. And after the father has traversed the hunting trails and explored the swamp, all in vain, he acquires the conviction that every step forth leads him fatally and inexorably to his son's corpse.

Not a thing to reproach himself, pitiful. Only the cold, terrible, and consummated reality: His son has died crossing a...

But where? How to find the place? There are so many wire fences and the forest is so, so filthy. Oh, very filthy! If one is the least bit careless crossing the wires with the rifle in hand...

The father stifles a scream. He has seen... rise in the air. Oh, it is not his son. No! Returns to another place, and another, and another.

Nothing will be gained from seeing the color of his flesh and the anguish in his eyes. That man has not called out to his son yet. His mouth remains mute though his heart clamors for him at the top of his lungs. He knows pronouncing his name, calling aloud to him, means confessing his death.

"Little one!" it escapes him suddenly. If the voice of a man of strong will can weep, let us mercifully cover our ears before the anguish clamoring in that voice.

Nobody and nothing respond. Following the red spikes of the sun, the father, who has aged ten years, searches for his recently deceased son.

"My son! Little one!" he clamors in a diminutive that rises from the depths of his body.

Before, when he was fulfilled and peaceful, that father endured hallucinations—his son falling, forehead opened by a chromium nickel bullet. Now, in every somber corner of the forest, he sees glints of wire; and at the foot of a pole, beside the fired pistol, his...

"Little one! My son!"

The forces that deliver a poor hallucinating father to the most atrocious nightmare have a limit. Ours feels them yield, when he sees his son course in from a side trail.

It suffices for a thirteen-year-old boy to see his father at a fifty-meter distance, recognizing his expression and that he is missing his axe in the forest, to run towards him with moist eyes.

"Little one..." murmurs the father. Exhausted, he allows himself to fall on the resplendent sand, wrapping his arms around his son's legs.

The creature, held this way, is rooted. As he understands his father's pain, he caresses his head slowly.

"Poor father."

In short, time has passed. It will be three soon. Father and son commence the return home together.

"Why didn't you track the time with the sun?" the first still murmurs.

"I did keep track, father. But when I was about to return, I spotted Juan's herons and followed them..."

"What you put me through, boy..."

"Pio pio," the boy still murmurs.

After a long silence, the father asks, "And the herons? Did you kill them?"

"No."

It is a trivial detail, after all. Under the red-hot sky and air, through the clearing in the espartillo grass, the man returns home with his son, on whose shoulder, which nearly reach the height of his own, rests his happy father's arm. Returns soaked in sweat and, though broken in body and soul, smiles, happy.

※ ※ ※

Smiles, hallucinating happiness. Since that father walks alone. He has found nobody and his arm rests on a void. Because behind him, at the foot of a pole and with legs raised, tangled in the barbed wire, his well-loved son lies under the sun, dead since ten that morning.

Lady Lioness

Once the weak, naked, clawless man dominated the other animals by exerting his intelligence, he began to fear for his species' fate.

He had reached the summits of thought and beauty. But under these exclusively intellectual triumphs, which cost him his beastly origin, the species was dying of anemia. After that relentless struggle, in which the mind exhausted all the dialectics, sophisms, cons, and bad intentions that fit in it, not one drop of sincerity remained in the human soul. And to restore the primordial freshness of the expiring human soul, the men mulled over introducing a being to the city, raising and educating among them a living example: a lion.

The city in question was naturally enclosed by walls. And from atop them the men enviously watched the animals with escaping foreheads and copious blood, run freely.

So, a committee went to meet the lions and said this to them, "Brothers, peace is our mission today. Hear us carefully and without fear. We come to solicit a young lioness to educate among us. We'll give you a human son as collateral, who you'll raise simultaneously. We wish to raise a day-old lioness. We'll teach her and, leading by example, her fortitude will benefit our children. When both are older, they'll freely choose their destinies."

The lions meditated with oblique eyes before that unordinary frankness for many hours. They finally accepted and thus, penetrated the desert with a three-year-old man whose slow pace they matched; meanwhile the men headed back to the city carrying with exquisite care, each in turn, a young lioness, so young she opened her pupils that morning, and fixed the clear and empty gaze of her blue eyes on each man that held her.

We will speak of the young man one day. Regarding the lioness, no praise suffices to describe the care she received. The entire city saw that weak being as an odd and divine messiah from whom they expected salvation.

The savage and tender pupil was raised and educated by hearts palpitating love. The gazettes did not report on the king's health as frequently as on the young beast's progress. The philosophers or rhetoricians never made such an effort to indoctrinate a soul in the divine mysteries of their art. Science, heart, poetry, everything was expected of her. And when the lady lioness was officially presented to the city in her first evening gown, the newspapers faithfully rendered, in exalted chronicles, the heart of the people.

The young lioness learned to talk, temper her movements, smile. She learned to wear human clothing, blush, meditate resting her chin on her hand. She learned as much as a beautiful daughter of man can and should. But, above all, she learned the divine art of singing.

We can no longer fully grasp the seductive style and grace of a young lioness who, dressed like a daughter of man, debuts in a salon, blushing shyness.

Because the most intimate intricacies of the human heart had never, in fact, found vocal expression in such an organ. Flow of a virgin soul, startled by poetry since its first dawn? Who knows! And that divine creature least of all, since it is lazy to note that she was educated into a human adolescent, with a woman's ideas, tenderness, and manners.

Meanwhile, as in her early childhood, the lady lioness garnered public attention. She was the hope of a people, every concert she announced awoke tumultuous exclamations of jubilee in the heart of the city.

With the first note, the inhabitants trembled in recognition: that voice exhaled their human souls. How could the savage creature thus express, better than them, the lyricism, hope, and cries, of a soul foreign to her own?

"A soul she didn't possess…"

This became, little by little, impressed on the city… Her supreme artistry was recognized; but the men raising a young lioness in their hearth had not sought the assimilation of their daydreams. No. They expected innate freshness, savage sincerity, a cry for freedom, in sum, everything the human soul lost in its exhausting mental race.

Her voice excelled at being exclusively "human." And more was demanded of her.

In this regard, the gazettes also expressed the general feeling: *At last night's concert, the supreme artist outdid herself again, and now we cannot but repeat the praise always bestowed in her honor. Nevertheless, interpreting popular sentiment, always ferociously addicted to our pupil, we declare the desire to hear a note in her divine voice, a single freshly intimate note that betrays her personality. Not one of her deepest accents is unknown to us. Presently the illustrious artist has interpreted the human soul magisterially; but only that. Excess "humanity", we dare accuse. We anxiously await the fresh freedom cry of her strange soul, sincere and unobstructed.*

We effortlessly believe the delicate artist could not have dreamt of a more unexpected and unjust blow.

"What have I done," she sobbed, "to be treated this way?"

"You're not to blame," they consoled her. "Your voice is always as pure as your heart, and we are as susceptible to your charm today as we were yesterday. But... the people are right in a sense. Your accent lacks some sincerity. You sing adorably, but the passion in your voice is a woman's."

"But I am a woman!" cried the inconsolable creature.

She rose to the stage trembling with emotion at her next concert. But below the always well-earned applause, she felt the withdrawn heart of the city.

"How's it possible," they noted, "not to give us a wild note of immense and free expression, the savage accent of your race, which our species has worn out and ignored for thousands of years? Let yourself go freely into your daydreams when you sing, forget everything you learned from us, and you'll give us a pure and supreme note of art."

"No... I can't... I can't!..." The artist shook her head.

The entire city gathered to hear the young lady again, in hope of a miracle; knowing the ardent demand made of her.

Trembling and uncertain, the young lady began singing. She felt, as she sang, the breath of the city held to her voice and remembered the hope invested in her. Closing her eyes, with supreme effort she erased the present from her memory; a warm breath swept her soul like a gale, and the young lady poured the awoken passion into one supreme note.

The room was still: that note of passion was a "roar." Purely and indisputably, the young lady had roared.

More surprised and spooked by her own voice than anyone: "I did it by accident..." She sobbed, "I don't know what happened!..."

Though mortally undeceived by the artist, the city in extraordinary concert offered her the opportunity to veil that fateful night. But when the artist, dominated by her art, turned to open those large oppressive doors to her soul, she roared again.

It was no longer possible. The city deliberated, though their hearts were torn, coldly.

We lament putting the hope of our race in one foreign

to ours. We raised a strange creature with more warmth than we granted our children. We infused her soul with the most exultant human qualities. And when we demanded the sincerest and freshest note from her voice... she roared.

And they escorted the poor creature to the city gates, she stumbled with each step and pressed her palms to implore pity.

The night had closed. The young lady walked robotically, penetrating the desert, until the warm wind tussling her hair in the dark opened her eyes. Her nose dilated widely as crude body odors without origin reached yet did not graze her; and then, she stopped, turned to face the city, and stripped. She took off her suit, everything that had disguised her primary condition, until she was nude. And then rooting herself with a rigid tail and hard phosphorescent eyes, the lioness roared.

For a long time, alone, and as if lengthened by the tension in her flanks, she roared towards the decrepit city, pressing the flanks to the skeleton, as if with each roar she finally sang freely and unobstructedly, the pure and deep voice of her virgin insides.

The Puritan

Cinematography sets, those film studios around which millions of faces rotate in an orbit of unsatiable curiosity and unrealizable daydreams, inherited from defunct painting studios the legend of lavish orgies on art's altar.

The free spirit characteristic of great actors, on one hand, and the bloated salaries they show off, on the other, explain those festivals whose sole objective is more often than not to maintain the vibrancy of public awe, before the fantastic, distant Hollywood stars.

Upon concluding daily tasks, the studio is deserted. Perhaps the technicians' workshops persist in their work all night; and about one or ten kilometers away, the day's commotion is prolonged in an Arabian Nights-themed party. But on set—specifically, in the studio—the greatest silence now reigns.

This silence and sense of desertion since weeks past are especially emitted by the central wardrobe, a vast hall whose entrance, so wide three cars fit through it, opens onto the interior patio, to the workshops' great sandy plaza.

To annul the damage of potential fires, the costume department is isolated behind the square and its great double doors are never closed. Through its open leaves, on clear nights, the moon invades great part of the dark hall.

In that enclosure, where not even the creaking of the film-developing machine reaches, in the dead of night we calmly hold our gathering of dead film actors.

✶ ✶

The photographic print on the tape, shaken by the speed of the machine, excited by the blazing light of the bulbs, galvanized by the incessant projection, has deprived our sad bones of the peace that should reign over them. We are dead, no doubt; but our annulment is not complete. An intangible second life, only warm enough not to freeze, rules and animates our specters. We wander peacefully through the wardrobe under moonlight, without anguish, passion, or memories. Something like a subtle stupor envelops our movements. We would resemble sleepwalkers, indifferent to each other, if the immediate shadow of the enclosure did not imitate the nondescript hall of a mansion, where the ghosts of what we were pursue a subtle parody of life.

We have not shaken the souls of the stars that survive us in vain; we have not let our heart sleep in their arms one hundred times so, our covert nocturnal meetings cannot discuss their new films. Our own past—life, struggles, and loves—is closed off from us. Our existence begins with the strike of a shutter. We are an instant: perhaps everlasting, but still a sole spectral instant. The film and projection that deprived us of eternal sleep, close off our World, offscreen, from all other interests.

※
※ ※

Our gathering, nevertheless, is not always attended by all the costume-department visitors. When one is absent, we know some film they acted in is being screened in Hollywood.

"He's sick," we say. "He stayed home."

The next night, or three, or four later, the ghost occupies his usual spot in the company he prefers. And though his countenance expresses fatigue and, in his silhouette, we perceive the fine ravaging of a new screening, neither betrays a trace of true suffering. One can say that during the time invested in the screening of his film, the actor was submitted to a semi-conscious dream.

※
※ ※

Something very different happened to Her (I refuse to name Her), the beautiful and vivid star who made Her entrance among us in the wardrobe one night—dead.

The success this actress experienced in Her lifetime, throughout Her brilliant and fleeting meteoric career, surprises no one. From woman, She took the richest qualities. Extreme beauty of face, body, and feeling—any one of these supreme gifts can turn into excess charm that breaks down a female soul. She possessed and bore all three, almost as a punishment.

She was bestowed everything during Her brief passage in the world. She knew the madness of success, fortune, vanity, flattery, and danger. She was only denied the madness of love.

Among all the men that submitted to Her, by Her side or traversing two thousand leagues with clamor and desire, She offered all of herself to the only being able to cast Her aside: a puritan with inviolable moral principles that invested his honor in his wife and tender ten-month-old son before meeting the actress.

It is not easy to guess the emotional state of a rancid lineage Quaker like Dougald Mac Namara; but no one would enjoy enduring the collision between austere principles and culprit love liberated in his heart.

She met him in the studio, since the lucky mortal was interested in cinema. And though She never offered him Her lips, She knew full well that if She had, he would have taken Her arms from his neck, the rigid and hard embodiment of duty. Sometimes the blond races bestow an admirable being upon the world, one eternally inscrutable to us with darker consciences and eyes.

She knew full well that he loved Her, not as a man, but as a martyr. And when a lover usurps all the heroism of love for himself, the other is only left with death.

In sum: the father figure, embittered to his feces, returned the sacred vessel of love She embodied and offered. And She, lacking the strength to endure it, killed herself.

As a suicide, in fact, She could not enjoy our tame peace, nor was She forbidden love and pain. Her heart always beat; and from Her deep set eyes we could not guess what dose of arsenic or mortal love still dilated them with anguish.

Because unlike what we endured, She led a half-life, faithfully suffering the passion of Her characters. When our films were screened, as I mentioned, we disappeared from the gathering. Not Her. She remained, lying there, bundled up in the cold, with an anxious and breathless expression. We pretended not to notice Her presence at those times; but She sat upright on the divan as soon as the projection concluded, and expressed Her own wreckage.

"Oh, what anguish!" She said uncovering Her forehead. "I feel everything I do, as if I hadn't feigned in the studio... Before, I knew that after finishing a scene, regardless of its intensity, I could think about something else and laugh... Now, I can't... It's as if I'm the character!..."

Well. We ended our days legally and owed them nothing. She cut short Her own. Her unfinished life faced a strong deficit, which Her cinematographic ghost charged, scene after scene, through Her supposedly faked pain...

Must pay. Of Her love, She said nothing, until the night She murmured bitterly after concluding Her task:

"If at least... If at least I couldn't see him!..."

Oh! To understand the poor creature's suffering, it is not needless to remember: night after night, after a month-long disappearance from Hollywood, Mac Namara attended all Her film screenings at the Monopole, he did not miss one. Until today, literature never captured what the husband, son, and mother of a deceased actor experience: the gravity of seeing one's lost loved one on screen, pulsing with life. Nor has anyone imagined a torture equal to Hers: the man who drove Her to suicide surrenders to Her love, but She cannot run deliriously into his arms, look or turn to him, because all of Her being and love are now no more than a cinematic specter!

It was not joy either that traversed the heart of the puritan, whose wife and son slept calmly, but whose open eyes contemplated the live actress. Some feelings cannot be given a verbal body but can be wholly followed with closed eyes. Dougald Mac Namara's belonged to this kind.

For us, nevertheless, only Her situation was of vivid interest. It is very sad to die in vain when life still demands what it can no longer receive.

"It isn't possible," She sometimes let slip after a trance, "to suffer more than me! Three quarters of an hour watching him in the audience!... And me, here!..."

Insensitively, we all forgot our walks under the moonlight and heatless chattering, to but contemplate that torment. We darkly intuited that She would not endure the tortures a cruelty without precedent inflicted on Her truncated life.

To die again! But never, never will one find rest who sought it surrendering beyond existence, buying the paralysis of love with handfuls of arsenic?

"Oh, to die!" She said, squeezing Her face between Her hands. "And never see him, never see him again!"

But on the opposite side of the screen, Dougald Mac Namara did not take his eyes off Her.

One night, at the sad hour, while She lay motionless on the divan, half-hidden by as many plaid blankets as we could toss on Her body, the young woman suddenly uncovered Her eyes.

"He's not here," She said slowly. "He didn't come today..."

The projection of the film continued but the actress did not suffer the passion of Her characters. Everything vanished into inert nothingness, leaving as compensation a path of livid and tremendous anguish that traveled from an empty seat to a spectral divan.

Dougald Mac Namara did not return the next night, the one after that, or on any that followed for a month.

Must I note that on those nights, as of half an hour before the screening, our lips became mute and, with the first screech of the film, our eyes did not abandon the patient?

She also waited (and how!) for the projection to begin. For a long time—time spent looking for him in the audience—Her face, drawn thin by suicide, wore a fantasy of anxious hope. And when Her eyes finally closed (Mac Namara had not left!) the agonizing flattening of Her features was only comparable to the prior delirium.

New nights followed in vain. The seat at the Monopole remained empty.

In an austere home on any tree-lined street, a man of rigid principles had to guard the sleep of his chaste wife and pure infant. When one has resisted a warm mouth that begged to be kissed, one can resist a dancing celluloid illusion just as well. After a moment of weakness, Mac Namara would not return to the Monopole.

We believed that. She no longer expressed Her desires to die; She was dying.

One night, finally, as the projection began, our eyes still fixed on Her countenance, Her dead hands ripped brusquely off Her eyes. Suddenly Her face brightened with joy, reaching the radiant splendor whose secret is life, Her arms outstretched and She cried out. Oh, God, what a cry!

"She's seen him," we said to ourselves. "He returned to the Monopole!"

Beyond. There, nowhere in the world, the rigidly principled puritan shot himself.

There is, thus, something above Death and Duty. Two steps away from us, now, the lovers embrace. They will never be apart. He suffocated his impure love, beat it temporarily by hiding in a theater, and finally returned triumphant to his austere home. Now he is beside Her on the divan.

She smiles almost fleshly joy, as pure as Her death. She now owes fate nothing and rests happily. Her life has ended.

His Absence

At the same pace that led me to the office a moment ago, with the same clothes and ideas, I rashly change direction and head to my wedding.

It is three in the afternoon on a summer's day. At this time, in broad daylight, I will surprise and marry my girlfriend. How do I explain this unexpected and terrible urgency?

I asked myself a thousand times the question that constitutes the darkest crevice in my soul; I afflicted my brain trying to clarify this: Why did I notice, seduce, and propose to my current girlfriend? By what impulse am I led at this pace in broad daylight on February 24, 1921, to fatally and urgently marry a woman who never heard my lips offer the remotest wedding date?

My girlfriend! I never hallucinated with her, nor suffered any related illusion. No one, but me, can fall in love with her. She is as ugly, rough, and thin as one can be. Films sometimes feature my girlfriend's type, a skeletal woman with straightened hair and the nose of a harpy. There is no other woman like her in the world. And this is the woman, among all others, that I have chosen as my wife.

But, Why? The strangeness, even monstrosity of this choice, never made me blush with shame. I watched but did not see her; I sleepwalked behind her; she made love to and will marry a man who sleeps with his eyes open.

But right now, as I see my life teeter on the edge of the abyss, Why don't I stop?

I cannot. I feel myself go, I must go at all costs, as if a rope drags me. I control all my faculties, I feel and reason normally; but a huge, ambiguous, and indifferent will precedes them and rules my soul.

Thus, I approach her house, seeing as in a dream, afar in space and time, the minute yet perceptible silhouette of a man like me walking under the burning sun. I see through that man's clothes: his desperate soul. He will marry a monster against his will. The disgust and horror of what he will do rise to his mouth and eyes. That man would give his life—the one he will lose soon—to stop himself. All the rebellion in that chained soul struggles to hold its life back from disaster. Nothing but a little willpower, a meager exercise of restraint, is needed to save him...

... And I still walk where the sun shines, a sleepwalker watching the minute silhouette of a desperate man that resembles me...

And with immense surprise I see: a lake, black mountains, and a frozen dusk. Am I crazy? A lake colored by the dusk, down there, a thousand meters under my feet. Towering mountains that seem cut out of the cold sky with Chinese ink. And in the whole ambit no other being but me stands before the silence.

But how does this happen? What fantastic spell transported me here in a second? Because I was about to marry a monster a second ago. (And the tranquility of this lake...) A moment ago it was... It is three in the afternoon! (And this frozen dusk...) And the fence of that cursed house is right there! (And this savage solitude crushes me like an iceberg...)

Reflect. Can a man accept divine intervention in jest? Can he ask himself as I have, What spell has brought me here? What fairy or genie performed this miracle? A man walking down the street in Buenos Aires in broad daylight is perfectly susceptible to being transported to a desert by a genius in the blink of an eye.

Alright: but all my awoken senses tell me that I am watching night fall on an abyss... When I am actually heading towards a monster's home! I immediately feel, almost materially, my body crossing the street; see the dazzling cobblestones; perceive a reasoning that initiated and concluded in that instant... And then, this landscape!...

I look down at my clothing and a shudder traverses my bone marrow: I am dressed for winter... I inspect my pockets: nothing I own belongs to me!...

Oh, finally! My ID is mine: Julio Roldán Berger. But this telegram?... I did not have it today... I tremble as I open it and read, *Enchanted by the flowers. We expect you promptly on the third. Father cannot attend the wedding.*

Come by any means. Your Nora.

From Nora, the monster! I look at the mournful lake and a second sigh dilates my soul: so, I remain unmarried! I am free forever! What mysterious force protectively ripped me from the damned arms that would suffocate me?

Protected?... But what am I? Why am I here? Do I lie dead under a car, perhaps hit while crossing the street, and is this landscape not of the world I was born in?

No! I finally hear something, a noise. It is a car horn. And turn to see a chauffeur walk towards me, he says, "I thought you got lost, Mr. Berger... The hotel lit its lamps, there'll be fog."

I speechlessly watch the chauffeur: lost?... Hotel?...

Well, I have not died. I am alive, I am a guest at a mountainside hotel, where I have lunch, speak, interact, move from here to there, everything in perfect form, as proven by the chauffeur's slightly excessive deference. Only...

I do not have the faintest idea of where the hotel is, who I know, what I do, or anything. I am truly and effectively dead. And though dead, I stumble after the chauffeur, already pretending that I endured a fall to excuse my confused ideas and the one thousand and one mistakes I surely make.

***

With a handkerchief tied to my forehead (pretext: I fell off a cliff last afternoon and momentarily lost my memory), last night I went past the hotel lobby and locked myself in my room, which I was led to by a female porter that ceaselessly pitied Mr. Berger, who even forgot his room number after the fall...

I spent a sleepless night more confused than the men of Babel. I do not want to see a doctor: I make do with ordinary scandals. But I endured my first surprise of the day while requesting a train schedule this morning at the station.

While the employee spoke, I managed to see a large paper calendar through the window.

"You run ahead of time here," I said pointing to the almanac.

"What?" the man asked.

"The calendar"

"What's wrong with the calendar?"

"Nothing... it's just running ahead of time."

"Ahead? 1927."

"No, 1921"

The man, doubting himself at last, glances back quickly.

"See," turning back to his numbers, "1927."

"No, 21," I repeated.

"Alright; leave me alone, sir!" the employee concluded, watching me. "If you're dissatisfied with the calendar, here's the complaint book."

So, I looked from the calendar to the man three times, and then walked slowly onto the platform.

1927! April 2, 1927! And the last memory I have dates to yesterday, February 24, 1921!

***

A man can go mad with far less. Mad, mad! That word dances like a ring of fire before my mental fog. Was I? Am I now? But no! Everything here contradicts… And I still notice, as I noticed in the chauffeur, a deference towards me that borders on admiration. Except for the ticket seller this morning…

The train leaves today. A day and a half from now I will be in Buenos Aires… if Buenos Aires still exists.

***

If I had any doubts in the hotel, upon arriving here in Buenos Aires I felt, in everything, the aged world. I have no sense of the 2,190 or so days of struggles, passions, and agonies gone by. I did not spend that time sick. Neither unconscious nor cataleptic. My body and soul lived. But I do not know what I thought and did for six years. My *I*, who I know and speaks now, is still on a sunny street, since February 24, 1921.

This morning I flew to my doctor's home in that state of mind. If I expected him to be taken aback, that did not happen. He was simply glad I made it there safely, he expected me. And looked at me as if I was not returning from a truly mortuary trip of six years.

The moment of understanding arrived.

"So, you expected me?" I said hesitantly, looking at his pupils.

"Of course! Your telegram was explicit," he answered.

"Oh! And it was mine?"

"I guess so."

"Julio Roldán Berger?"

"Come on!..."

"No, no!" I said, "The situation is graver than you think. Answer exactly what I ask, as if I know nothing. How long ago did you last see me?"

"Alright: fifteen days ago."

"Why?"

"Because you were in Lago Negro."

"On the range?"

"Of course. Now allow me..."

"No, don't ask me anything yet. Please, Campillo! Look at me and answer frankly: Over these past six years, did you notice anything abnormal about me?"

"Nothing."

"Nothing?"

"No, nothing! Nothing! How many times do you need

me to repeat it? Come on, Berger!"

"Just a few more. And I was never ill... gravely ill?"

"No."

"And... I was never... mad?"

Then, the doctor's expression changed.

"Don't worry, I'm not mad now," I said. "Look and you'll see... But, before? Campillo, my friend!..."

But the psychiatrist did not seem annoyed by my idiotic questionnaire anymore. He made me sit across from him and calmly said, "I won't ask anything; tell me what you wish."

"Alright! We'll understand each other that way. I'll begin. My last memory of my thoughts, actions, life date back to the day before yesterday."

"A fall..."

"I fell nowhere. My day before yesterday was?"

"I don't know."

"February 24, 1921. That's what's wrong."

Campillo stepped back to take a better look at me, and I stood up with my hands in my pockets.

"You heard right," I concluded coldly. "The day before yesterday, as I crossed the street, about to step onto the road, I found myself on the mountain range with the purple lake at my feet and enveloped by the cold of dusk, concluding the very reflection that I began a second earlier as I hovered above the road. And seemingly six years passed from one moment to the next. How? I'd like you to explain."

And the explanation finally arrived, after infinite insidious questions from the doctor. Here, thus, is what happened.

I belong to a family of nervous people, some hysterics and even an epileptic grandmother prospered. I personally never endured any nervous or mental disorders, excepting the abnormal affective state I described, at the start of 1921.

Yet then my grandmother's epilepsy suddenly awoke, it dodged crises and dramatic attacks but submerged me abruptly into an *absence*, smack-dab in the middle of that sweltering street. Under the influence of this epileptic state which the sufferer does not perceive in the slightest, life continues as always. Except that at the end of a day, month, year, the man awakes abruptly. He finds himself in a place he does not recognize, nor does he know why he is there, nor does he know anyone, nor does he retain even a slight recollection of what he did after he fell into that epileptic fugue. His last memory dates to that moment; of the rest: the triumphs or tragedies of his own life, he knows nothing. In other words, during those months or years the man has been dead. He lived, loved, howled with pain, or raved with joy, but was dead. Another man continued living in his name, body, and soul; but he himself is detained, suspended on the edge, about to step on the road... to awake six years later, amazed and idiotic before his absurd existence.

"That's the case," concluded the psychiatrist. "And don't complain too much because there are epileptics that set out on a walk one day and don't stop until they reach the pole. Others head straight to the sea or traverse a fire. You're one of the lucky ones."

"From your cynical point of view, perhaps," I answered with a shrug, going to the window to rest my forehead on the glass.

But my friend descended from his scientific high horse.

"Come on, Berger! I more than realize what's going on... I'm too fond of you to abuse our friendship by mocking you. What'll you do?..."

"But that's precisely what I'm asking you!" I became peeved, "What do I do now? What was I doing in Lago Negro? What have I done over the past six years? Who do I ask to account for my life then and how do I account for my actions? You can't imagine, despite all your definitions, what it's like to ignore how you performed your life for six years! I only know I did one thing... the one thing I shouldn't have!"

And I added, smiling with almost dismal joy, "What a nightmare, my friend! You were in Europe then and didn't hear... I was going to be married. I now understand that my epilepsy began when I looked at that woman, followed her and put a ring on her finger, like a sleepwalker... At the last moment I became aware of what I was about to do, as I was crossing the street under that sun of fire... And then I saw the lake. But I had her telegram, she only spoke of marriage. How could my second soul remain attached to such a monster, while the first stayed suspended above the road? How haven't I?..."

"Wait a moment!" my friend interrupted, who watched me, becoming estranged. "What was your monster's name?"

"Nora. I still have her telegram."

And while Campillo read it: "And to think," I repeated joyfully, "if I didn't put down roots on the road, I'd be married tomorrow!"

"You will be," the doctor said calmly, handing me the note back. "You're getting married tomorrow."

"To Nora?... Huh! Now you're the crazy one."

"I'm not. You're marrying Nora... Strindberg tomorrow."

Another tableau vivant. One and another grew still, watching each other.

"As I said," Campillo finally interrupted with a smile. "That telegram is not from the... monster, but your current girlfriend, Nora Strindberg. You've been courting her for a year. You were supposed to be wed fifteen days ago, but you were called away to the range on a time-sensitive issue. The wedding was postponed until tomorrow, April 5. You sent her a magnificent basket of orchids, so I must warn you that you're madly in love. This telegram that refers to her father's absence is Nora's response. Everything is perfectly arranged for the wedding, tomorrow at three. And if I can recount these details, it's because we became closer during your six-year epileptic absence than you suppose, and I'm now your best man. That's the case.

I stopped hearing him, desperate. Another Nora! Did my fate consist of nothing but planning absurd marriages and becoming stupefied when crossing a road? Did six years of epilepsy not purge the abjection of my soul when I fell in love with the first Nora, by the time this second monster came to fill the miserable hole in my new heart?

"No, a thousand times no!" I stood again, "One Nora suffices; I don't want another. If you'd seen her! You'll never see a more horrible woman, believe me! And this one must be…"

"Wait another moment! Don't speak yet," Campillo jumped. "I have her portrait, because we're also close friends… Here it is, look."

I set the photograph down at a distance, suspicious, but as I peered down, my eyes widened.

"This is…" I murmured.

"Nora Strindberg. You can study her. You'll see her better by the window."

I went to the window and moved the lace curtain aside. For a long time, I contemplated the trembling, smiling face I held in my hands, whose eyes seemed to close more as she stared back.

Campillo smoked without turning away, and I remained immobile and mute, like a poor devil the doors of paradise open to but does not dare enter.

"That's Nora Strindberg," Campillo said at last with a

trace of irony. "What do you say?"

"Beautiful," I murmured. "I've never seen a woman with a gaze as naïve and passionate..."

"Very good, naivety and passion. And the rest? Face shape, nose, mouth?"

"Unique in a woman born human... But the expression, above all. How old is she?"

"Nineteen. She isn't old."

I stopped listening. Something absurd, impossible, looms over me in the shape of a question.

"And this person..." I finally risked without looking away from the portrait, "is in love with me?"

"Very much. Mad for you, that's the phrase. Study her closely.... She'll be your wife by this time tomorrow."

It is not worth remembering the one thousand anxious questions I asked my friend. I moved naturally from surprise to surprise with each response. Until the cup overflowed when I finally exclaimed, like any man that excuses himself from an undeserved fortune, "But what have I done, poor devil of an engineer, to deserve that creature's love?"

"I suppose she partly loves you for you," Campillo answered. "And partly for circumstances you still ignore. Didn't you say you noticed others treat you obsequiously, too respectfully?"

"That's right," I answered remembering the air of mystery with which I was observed in the hotel and here, in Buenos Aires, which I attributed to the stigma of madness and idiocy impressed on my countenance.

"Alright," the psychiatrist proceeded taking a book from the library and offering it to me. "The other reason for Nora's affection is this book. Read the title."

And I read: *The Open Sky* by Julio Roldán Berger.

"And this?" I murmured, imprisoned by stupor.

"It's your book. See the date: 1924."

"But what is it about?"

My friend couldn't help but smile upon hearing that question from the stupefied author's lips.

"Its subject doesn't fit any definition. You can call it philosophy of humanity… Essays of Emersonian, Maeterlinckian… philosophy. I don't know! The truth is that it's simply a work of genius. Do you understand, my friend? By a genius. It's a shame you don't remember, realize the resonance of your book."

"But I can't have written this!" I exclaimed reaching the cusp of disquiet, "I don't understand writing, not a word! And philosophy, if only!"

"And yet it's so, regardless. 'In your book there is,' I'm quoting the aces of the genre the world over, 'an unexpected vision of Life,' just as it sounds, with a capital 'L.' 'No one in the world of the living has ever seen what you describe as the fate of humanity, the reason for its terror, and its miserable yearning for serenity.' I continue to speak to you as a critic. In Europe and the United States at first no one wanted to believe that eclosion could take place in the mind of an Argentine, a South Americano... They were convinced, and here you find yourself transformed, two years ago now, into the most celebrated writer of all time. That's why people look on astonished to find a man of your intellect beside them or passing by.

※
※ ※

What can I respond? I held in my hands, like ashes, a work that was deep, transcendental, unique in the world, which I meditated, planned, and resolved at last in three hundred pages. And I completely ignored what it said.

I must warn, making my absurd situation understood, that I never concerned myself with the fate of humankind or anything of that kind. I spent a lifetime working to get ahead, and never saw in other men anything but comrades in the struggle, more or less energetic, more or less incapable, but all willing to elbow me out of the race if I did not overtake them, chest ahead. I made myself a free man without anyone's help, and if I am not an intellectual in the common sense given to that word, I worked my fingers to the bone engineering dams in the North. I also know the value of a human soul tested ruthlessly. I know the hunger of the student, and the hunger of someone with only a day and night ahead to build the pillar that threatens to collapse under an avenue of unexpected water. I know better than others the energy held in the only heart of a man responsible for a vast structure. But it never occurred to me to write about this or the fate of life.

Noting this, thus, Where did my book come from?

"From within you," the psychiatrist tells me. "Don't forget that you're epileptic. Epileptics are not all gifted, but geniuses abound among them. It's the *sacred malady.* Among genius epileptics the normal function of their brains is to think ingeniously, like oysters whose illness produces pearls. You needed to be absent for your brain to become 'ill' and write this book. It's clear."

Something always seemed dark to me.

"And Nora?" I asked, "Does she like my book?"

"Your girlfriend? I told you. Your philosophy has a place in her love for you. Imagine! You're a great man."

I took the portrait from him again and again went by the window. Before the divine treasure that by a twist of fate would belong to me the next day, I meditated... And came to a resolution.

"Here is your photograph," I said, returning it to Campillo. "I won't marry."

"Huh?"

"I won't marry."

"But are you mad? You believe she doesn't deserve you? That's enough to..."

"Don't say stupidities, Campillo... I won't marry because I shouldn't. She doesn't want me; but the author of that..." I pointed to the book over my shoulder.

"But you're him, damn it! Absent or not—and only we know about that—you thought and wrote *The Open Sky*."

"I didn't; we also know that."

"Come on!... If a musician dreams a melody and writes it down when he wakes, it doesn't stop being his? Come on, Berger! Take the happiness you're offered, otherwise you'll be the worst imbecile... and criminal. What right do you have to reject the love of a girl like Nora? Your damn book? Who says you won't begin to philosophize again and write another, better still? Don't you always have your mind? Do you or not?... Then? *The Open Sky* required a mental jolt born from your absence. Why can't the emotional jolt of possessing Nora exalt it again? What do you know of the forty-thousand ways a man of your character seduces a girl like Nora? Do you believe you're unable, as you are, to be loved by a woman?"

"Depends. I always worked my fingers to the bone..."

"And because you worked so hard, you believe that Nora cannot want you for you. Bah! You can fast for two days, watching your dams dance under floods; but you don't understand what a man needs to drive a skirt crazy. What do you say?"

"I say nothing..."

"That's what I want to hear. Now let's create a campaign plan because in your state..."

"Precisely! Of this; I want to talk. What did I do over the past six years? What did I commit to?"

"I can't believe it. A man is who he is, even under the effect of alcohol."

"But I was under the effect of epilepsy, which is far worse."

"But in you. In you it was a larval state, let's call it that. You stopped in the street and gave way to another man who was you, in a distinct manifestation. The engineer with a hard head and muddy breaches was left immobile, mute, and white, suspended above the road for six years. Your replacement was an intellectual, a writer with an extraordinary vision, that fulfilled his fate with a bolt of genius and sunk into the fog of absence to give way to the original occupant. But one and the other are you. Over the past six years I was your close friend, close enough to be sure there is no infamy in any crook of your intimate life. A man with a clean heart in the eyes of a friend, not soiled by concealed nastiness. A man of action or thought, you'll always be Roldán Berger. If this is what you were missing to decide, be satisfied now.

And now, regarding Nora, there are reasons you don't see clearly. How do you propose we proclaim with great fanfare that due to an extraordinary case of epilepsy you ceased being yourself for six years, and you were dead when you wrote the book? Who'd believe it, and what would we gain from this cheap scandal? Let's remain, thus, naturally reserved about a case which would interest clinicians at most. And now what's your excuse for breaking your engagement to Nora one day before the wedding. You've been the most tender lover to her. She adores you—though the expression is idiotic—and her family has a weakness for you. The world—as they say in polite society—embraced your engagement affectionately. Both young, in love, free in their tête-à-tête, with the freedom granted by your name and her Scandinavian origin. And now, my friend: What's your excuse for breaking up the day before your wedding?"

A long pause, I watched Campillo watch me for a response.

"Alright," he finally said. "Now you see that it won't be easy. Listen to my conclusion. Nora is worth, her generous and enthusiastic heart alone, more than you suspect. I'm not speaking of her appearance; you saw that someone could die to conquer a face, eyes, and body like hers. You won't, in God's lifetime, find a creature equal to her within reach. The fondness of a cute girl picked up off the street would satisfy you. And yet Nora Strindberg loves you madly and there is no greater joy for her than to become yours. I'm done."

As his seduction plea concluded, my last scruples vanished. How to discard an open sky (far more open than the one I described), whose cost of entry is only oblivion?

Forget, remember... Remember that behind my one-day intellectual splendor, I had a heart like any other, already beating beside Nora's chest...

"As you paint this picture," I finally agreed, "I forget everything... But one thing, to conclude, Why is it urgent for us to marry tomorrow? Why not wait a while, until?..."

"Until what? What would you gain from waiting? To fall so deeply in love that you'll kill me for not allowing you to marry earlier? Then, take swift action, Berger. Everything is perfectly ready for tomorrow, as it's been for months. And the little displeasure... One doesn't play with wedding dates, my friend... Especially when Nora is the one marrying, and she is desperate to rid herself of her last twenty-two hours as a single woman... I mean, of not being yours."

Only twenty-two hours... I gave in.

It escapes no one that my situation required one thousand precautions. First, I was informed of the state of my home (I flew from the station to see Campillo), of my new relationships, of my current social sphere; disregarding the thorniest issue: Nora and her family.

Campillo and I fixed everything in two hours of work. Suffering a fall to excuse my complete ignorance, remained the best pretext. In a few days, discerning behind my vacant eyes, I would assume the general lines of my new life; and with the pretext of amnesia at hand, there was no question, regardless of how nonsensical, I could not ask.

Regarding Nora, it would be prudent to let her know of my fall soon. She would run to see me, I would await lying on the divan, with a good towel on my forehead.

Campillo would not allow me to speak, giving me time to orient myself, especially among the people Nora may drag with her. Concluding, thus, the last touches to the scene, Campillo's telegram was sent, while he continued informing me of what I missed.

* * *

From what my friend learned, on February 24, 1921, and on the days prior any abnormality in me was unnoticeable, no one noticed. I possibly ceased seeing the horrible woman I was engaged to. She possibly wrote me one or one thousand letters until I saw her. It is not difficult to imagine that I went and after hearing her violently enraged recriminations, as one hears the rain, dropped the ring in a corner, and walked out, my back burning with curses. Perhaps I did that, but I cannot remember.

From the beginning of 1921 to 1923 I led a regular life, not a single event set apart from the norm. Campillo received my letter in 1921, dated in Neuquén, and did not notice the smallest change in my ideas or sensibilities. I often returned to Neuquén for work, and during my stays in Buenos Aires, I resumed my friendship with Campillo, who returned. But I do not remember it either.

It apparently occurred to me to write at the start of 1924. I fled to the South again, but not to work this time, and returned in December of that year with *The Open Sky* manuscript. I gave it to Campillo, but he did not wish to read it, convinced that, only after professional writers, engineers and doctors are the worst authors.

I published the book and its success astonished Campillo. My colleagues here grew silent; but when the reflections on my book arrived from the other hemisphere, saying of me what has not been said of anyone since Kant, the whole country was stupefied. All the anguish and hope in humankind was expressed in *The Open Sky*. It is very well possible; that I am ignorant of every word.

My triumph was definite. I was given a unique space in our intellectual world, and forgetting the dikes, aqueducts, and masonries, I gave myself over to the intellectual activities I could no longer abandon. At least that is what they all believed, and so did I. I had to descend to speak at conferences, so part of the intent of *The Open Sky* did not escape its readers completely.

As I finished one of these talks the family of a wealthy foreign financier, who settled in the Americas years ago, rose to meet the author of such a book. Who truly dragged the family there was their only daughter. Campillo says that the girl's excitement for my philosophy rose to her eyes and beat in her chest while she spoke. Mutual sympathies led me to her home days later and that is how I met Nora Strindberg. The rest: assiduous visits, even more assiduous encounters, love and the rest, all that is unlike any other.

Now I wait for her.

*
* *

... She left a moment ago. Everything I had an hour ago remains mine... In addition to a life of ignored joy, a whole year of unknown love, conquered with one kiss!

... I feel her willful voice in the hall, knocking down the doorman. I hear her anxiously questioning the doctor, who tries to halt her entry in vain. I finally feel her on me, and I still feel the freshness of her hands on my temples, and the kiss of her mouth that shakes me like an engine.

My friend! Julio! Answer me! Campillo, tell him to look at me!... Julio! My love!

I must only remain with my eyes closed for a moment. I opened them to find four fingers away the selflessly anguished eyes of a woman I was seeing for the first time, and as I smiled, they strayed with passion and joy.

"My beloved! It's over! What's wrong? A fall?... And Campillo wouldn't tell me anything! It's nothing, right? Tell me, Julio!"

"Yes, a fall, Nora... But it's nothing. In time I'll be fine."

And in a softer and slower voice, "How I wanted to see you!..."

"And I you!"

"My Nora..."

As you will see, I behaved in a convincing way. But behind my warm words I analyzed that unknown face coldly, whose cheek had once, nevertheless, or a thousand times rested against mine.

"Did you think about your Nora much? No, don't raise your voice! Murmur to me."

"Yes, my love…" Her eyelashes are denser than in the portrait…

"So did I. Did you receive my telegram in time? My poor love, what a fall!"

"I fell… It's been so long since I last saw you!…" She must look divine with her temples uncovered…

"Now yes, my beloved… Together forever! All yours, always! Campillo, mother: look away. Another kiss, a light one, the last one. It won't hurt you?"

"Let's try…" And if her mouth is paradise ajar, the humidity of her lips and her interior silk…

… I was dizzy and my heart, after a spasm, beat tumultuously. My last scruples were volatized in the flame of the love of a year that trembled in her fallen eyelashes upon offering me her mouth, which I rediscovered in a single kiss.

What else? The doctor finally intervened.

"It's nothing for concern," he said taking off my towel. "A slight commotion, of which there'll be no trace tomorrow. All that'll be left is the confusion of memories that already burden him. Can you believe he didn't recognize me when I entered? He stood and looked at me as if we'd never met."

Nora's anguish was reborn, while the mother (not hard to recognize), observed everything with suspicion.

"How odd! Berger doesn't recognize anyone?"

"Mother, he recognized me right away!"

"Well other than... But me, Berger, do you recognize me?"

"Not much," I dared, smiling. "I recognized you a moment ago."

"How odd!" the woman went on. "And if this happens to someone with his talent, what would be of us?"

"We'd surely die," Campillo agreed, very satisfied with the turn things were taking. "If I didn't recognize Mr. Strindberg tomorrow, I'd go straight to an insane asylum. Berger in contrast has the faculties to do so with impunity, the life of the author of *The Open Sky* cannot be dictated by the laws that apply to other men.

Upon the sudden evocation of my book, I felt a cold wave, a gust of freezing wind sweep my soul. And was left mute, my brow furrowed, so much so that the dignified lady solemnly concluded, "You're right, Campillo. His brain does not account to us what occurs within..."

And she watched me with deep maternal pride.

I was already standing and Nora Strindberg rested both her hands on my shoulders, recounting endlessly the one thousand and one preparations for the next day. And when at last she left, with the promise confirmed and sealed with a kiss, that within three hours she would be in her home, I let myself fall on the divan, holding my head, "This is absurd, Campillo, all horribly absurd... But if I don't marry her, I'll die."

⁂
⁂ ⁂

I did not die, Nora has been my wife for three months. If the joy of a home, extreme love, and the charms of a beautiful creature in your arms constitute the joy of a man, I am happy. My friend was a thousand times right: I never dreamt of a happiness equal to the one laid out before my eyes, my Nora's lips and warm heart. Campillo often repeats to me: and, which honors his character, I believe he and a hundred others ardently desired this palpating treasure which Nora Strindberg handed to me.

Now well, How can this love story continue if the same man carries it out in two stage, whose fortune culminates at this moment?

But I am unhappy. There is a being in this world, a ghost that demands and absorbs, behind my heart, the gazes, kisses, and warmth of my Nora's heart. This ghost is the author of *The Open Sky*. I tell myself in vain that we are one person; since otherwise, my wife would have pulled away from me the day after we married, turning me into an intruder stealing a foreign treasure. But I never noticed the slightest suspicion in her. She was and remains with me a living tenderness, as she was on our wedding night. My heart has not inflicted the slightest disabuse on her. She has not felt the slightest chill of inhibition upon having her soul lie beside mine.

But I am unhappy. Though I suppressed all intellectual

social activity, where I am and wherever I turn my eyes, there are always two people still watching me and one of them says to the other dissimulating his mouth with his hand, "He's the author of *The Open Sky*."

Every delivery from Europe includes dozens of books dedicated to the master. My name is mentioned at least once in every transcendental publication. Of every twenty words said to me, seven must be: "Will you write the sequel to *The Open Sky*?" And fourteen more times I feel atop my virgin fate of yesteryear, the overwhelming weight of my fatal intelligence.

I have answered hundreds of thank you letters. I attend conferences in universities and intellectual centers. I carry out, essentially, in the best way possible, my heavy responsibilities as a man of a genius.

As hard and idiotic as this disguise might be, I would accept it delightedly if the dignity of my love was not involved. I already mentioned Nora's enthusiastic reception of *The Open Sky*. She memorized everything that said of me and collects in a magnificent album thousands of clippings about the extraordinary book. Never has a woman been prouder of her husband's talent. She is the one that opens the pages of magazines feverishly, and skims the interminable studies of *The Open Sky*. And she, at last, runs radiantly to teach me.

On these occasions I am usually at my desk mentally revising some heavy calculation of materials. When left alone, sometimes I robotically take my own book from the shelf and open it anywhere.

Impossible! If there is something in the world that I do not understand it is my own book. At the second page I stop reading, as fatigued as if convalescing from a flew. My own work! My own thoughts! Can this be? Is there in them the effort of a genius unparalleled in the world since Kant. But I understand nothing and grow desperately bored with the reading.

* * *

Another month passed. I am unhappy—I repeat it to exhaustion. And so is she, Nora. For a month now the shame of this farse rises to my face, of this cloud of incense that envelops me as I move, it follows and flatters me like I am a genius clown. I rarely leave home; I spend all day at my desk with the doors closed and the light on, or bent over my old plans, with the resistance table in view. I go down to eat, go out at night for a short walk, and that is all.

But, after that sedative solitude in which I finally find myself, I feel my home and my happiness fall apart. Nora has taken me desperately in her arms, "Julio! This has gone on for ten days! Tell me what's going on!"

I caress her, frozen in place, "It's nothing, Nora... I'm sick..."

But she recoils from my touch, "It's not true! Julio, my

love! What have I done? We got married four months ago and now!..."

And falls on the divan, sobbing for her lost happiness.

But what can I say! How do I muster the strength to kill her and myself, saying that I am but the thief of another man's glories, and that what she loved passionately is a divine ghost atop the vulgar figure of a dam constructor?"

* *
*

And I? Do I deserve, perhaps, this bitterness of coldly obliterating the integral and pure happiness I found in my Nora's arms? Must I do it? I am a sick man, or I was six years ago. I have dressed as a peacock for the past three months, concealing the muddied boots of an engineer under my plumage. But I cannot steal the love that my girlfriend felt for me, with her eyes fixed on my forehead...

* *
*

... Concluding, thus. Last night—as I have done for the past month—I received the mail and separated the letters one by one. There were many letters. I went through it all slowly by the fire—very slowly... And finally called to my wife.

"Listen to me, Nora," I said, once she sat beside me. "I also feel that this situation is unsustainable. We cannot continue this way."

"Yes, yes!" she murmured anxiously and happily, taking my hands, "I couldn't any longer. Oh, Julio!..."

Her knees met mine, and her divine heart opened to my chest. And I felt in the firmness of her fingers and moistness of her gaze, the immensity of what I was about to lose. But I was already standing; I went to the table and returned with a copy of *The Open Sky*.

"This is the reason for my attitude," I said, handing her the book. "This book carries my name. But I didn't write it, Nora..."

Though my soul was frozen and my, heart torn, I did not mistake the horror Nora's eyes expressed.

"No," I said with a dead man's smile, "I haven't stolen it... I wrote it. But now (Do you hear me?) I know nothing of what I wrote. Remember nothing... I don't understand a word written there. You don't understand, do you? I didn't understand it either. I was sick... Campillo explained it all to me. I spent six years in an abnormal state, I was and wasn't always myself, nevertheless... I wrote the book then. I never wrote anything before... When I came to in myself... When I awoke from that six-year dream... it was April 2," I concluded, getting up.

Anguish... nothing but the most intense anguish in Nora's eyes.

"Three days before?..." She murmured shuddering and watching me.

In that shudder I only saw the repulsion with which the deepest fibers of her being rejected me. And I continued, my mouth and soul were desperately bitter:

"Yes, three days before our wedding... Now I ask myself how I mustered the disgrace to deceive you! Campillo told me everything. He helped me carry out the deception... But I alone am to blame. I saw your portrait... Campillo described you... After you came to see me... The only thing I should have done then—show you in the flesh the poor devil that I am—I didn't. I deceived myself. I deceived everyone, for... for your love. But I've stopped. It's too late, I know; horribly late... but forgive me. Confessing is as hard for me as forgiving will be for you... because I'm losing you! I know it well. Author of *The Open Sky*! A man of genius! Oh, no! I assure you not! I haven't written a word, less so about the fate of life. I lived to work my fingers to the bone, since I was twelve years old... The little I'm worth I owe to my will to make myself a man. I ask myself again how I could deceive you, steal your love... How did I think you could love me for me, though I'm not an intellectual... Yes, I wanted to speak to you, tell you... But it was foolish to do so, I now see that well. I lose you forever, I know! Forgive me, if you have the strength. I... I'll go now forever."

Oh, no! Why was a hand suddenly holding mine; it pulled her up—Nora stood by me.

"Where are you going?" she asked with slow anguish.

"My Nora!" my heart had the strength to cry out. "Is what you're saying true?"

"Where are you going?" she repeated wrapping her arms around my neck, while her body leaned against mine with the rigidity of a stone.

No, I did not leave! I did collapse with her on the divan, and sunk my head into her knees while she spoke, combing her hand through my hair.

"No, don't leave... You're mine... mine..."

And I, from the divine pillow...

"Nora... my adored, Nora... I'm not worthy of you..."

"Quiet... don't speak."

"Yes, it's true..."

"Sh!... Don't speak at all..."

And with still haunted eyes, fixed on the fire, turned pale by the effort of suffocating the sobs she could not release: "Don't speak... My darling... Don't move... My love..."

*
* *

"Do you believe you cannot, as you are, be loved by a woman? What do you know about seducing a woman like Nora?"

Campillo's words materialize lucidly to me as I finally hold *my* wife in my arms.

"You made me suffer so!" she meditates aloud before

the chimney fire we both contemplate. I sit on the divan; she sits... on air.

I add, "Losing the author of *The Open Sky* won't weigh on you?"

"Who?" asked Nora with feigned perplexity. "I don't know that gentleman. I only know..."

And what her lips don't utter, her eyes and mouth do in the form of an anxious and oppressed secret.

And as if this truly severe testimony did not suffice, Nora gets up and takes *The Open Sky* from the shelf, returns to sit on my knees, and with her arm around my neck, she tears the pages from the book, one by one, and throws them into the fire, which we watch burn in wonderment.

"Now," she says, bringing her free arm to join the one that intoxicates me, "that gentleman is dead..."

"And the public?" I recall, suddenly alarmed. "What will the public say, they expect the sequel to *The Open Sky?*"

"The public?" she answers. And speaking atop my own breath, "Let them wait..."

Nora is right. I am profoundly busy. Let the public... wait.

Beauty and the Beast

Her

Young female author seeks literary correspondence with colleagues. X. X. 17, newspaper office.

Ça and est. I am the author.

Before taking this step, I thought about it. The inconvenience of an anonymous correspondence, as you can imagine, is not what held me back until today. Thank God, I am above such pettiness. But the consequences of the correspondence unsettle me.

As a general rule, for sensitive women, in writing man is far more dangerous than in speech. He is ten times more eloquent. His notes of sweetness are untraceable. He does not impose his masculine presence. Looks away: before a pleasing woman, the gaze of the most cautious man is an insult.

This, in general. Specifically, only one kind speaks as they write; and these are the men of letters. The female soul of every writer provides a tact whose due value they never appreciate. They know our weaknesses; value as in themselves the plenitude of our joy and total vacuum of our disquiet. They reach our spirit without touching our flesh. Among all men, only they know how to be forgiven for being male.

Masculine crudeness... without the ideal spark that turns a thug into a poet, we would have returned to the caves or committed suicide. The feeling, tenderness, tact of men... Ugh! If I dared define love, I would say that for us it is hope and for them, need. Before this evidence it would not be worth living, if some of the small naked things the Lord drops in mothers' arms did not become great poets.

My God! It is hard to find them! I know them all from photographs and some, up close. But how fleeting this *close*! Dora's mother insists I visit on Wednesdays. Her living room is a true literary salon, as in the divine times of Princess Matilde. I can speak to them there, delight in their conversation, delight in the abandon of soulfully surrendering to them all of life in an instant.

Why don't I attend? Since I began this diary, I felt that sooner or later I would record this circumstance... angrily. I do not wish to be misinterpreted: being as young and beautiful, my face and figure, as they all say, flatters me. No, I do not err on the side of hypocrisy. But I emanate, what resembles, a particular seduction, a deep and blind attraction that surpasses my beauty, and deeply... disturbs.

"You soul is as pure as an iris," my aunt once told me. "But your fate is more fatal: to drive men mad."

"But what lies in me, aunt?" I nearly sobbed. "I don't provoke!"

"On the contrary! Because there isn't a drop of provocation in you, you attract like the abyss. Men aren't so dumb."

My God! What to do? Everywhere, in all my male friends and strange men alike, the same tangible blunder, the same crude incomprehension of the female soul. They believe one thing suffices to conquer our fine sensibility: being a man. How proud they are of that!

After God made woman, the golden key to her spirit was cast to mystery. The first suicide poet found it in his coffin; ever since, writers, its exclusive owners, hand it down.

I do not know the name of the artist that possesses it today; but I go to him, trusting.

I showed my aunt the ad I sent to the newspaper this morning. She put on her glasses, less so to read than peer over them at me.

"And have you considered the risk of liking one... not spiritually?" she asked.

"Oh, aunt!" I answered, sitting on the arm of the sofa to hug her. "If he's a writer, I'm his!"

Him

I may be the happiest man on earth. When I lost all hope, I finally found her! No one can imagine having within reach the charming passerby that drove us mad. I asked about her for three months; all in vain. And it is here that I find her, when I least expect it, on a Wednesday at the Morán's.

Coincidence places me, upon entering, before Mrs. Morán, who professes cordial esteem for me. And is your aunt!

"Magnificent," I say, "do me a great favor: introduce me."

"You like her?"

"I'm mad about her."

"Then lose hope. She isn't for you."

"Why? I'm not irremediably vile."

"You're charming; but you're not the man that calls to Mechita's heart."

"Damn! She is that unconquerable?"

"For you, immensely."

My friend does not seem to mock me. I murmur, "Truly?" with such a grave accent and inconsolable expression that the lady, after sizing me up in silence, takes pity."

"I care madly about Mechita, but also hold you in high esteem. You're sure you can make her happy one day?"

Damn Mechita! Before such solemnity, and the superhuman exaltation of Mechita, he asked fearfully, "But she's a woman... like any other?"

"Don't be mad," my friend answered, "I mean, can you fall in love... with her spirit?"

"If her spirit possesses a hundredth part of her physical charm, I'll marry her tomorrow."

"You'll find out for yourself. Because I hold you in such esteem, I'll be unfaithful to Mechita. Come closer and listen."

And with the ensuing surprise, I was made privy to the secret ad to appear in a newspaper, so I may act accordingly to my convenience.

Her

Done. Total success. I received eight responses, eight spiritual letters on stationery. Three are monogramed and four begin like ours, on the last page.

But what letters! My God! If I was born a poet and a man, I believe I could not match their finesse.

Them? Not all. Seven letters are the same, but the last is an enigma. Firstly, it is written on a vulgar page torn from a notebook. Secondly, it gives the impression that the author does not know what a literary correspondence is: "*...to the extent of my strengths, I delight in striving to flatter you...*"

What style! "Trying to *flatter* me..." Its author has an artistic vocation, insofar as he believes he is one; but nothing else, poor thing...

I waited ten days to answer any. See why:

Writers, due to their prodigal feelings, receive many feminine letters, not all are inspired by artistic emotion. The least discerning of my eight writers continues suspecting me of such a bond.

My silence will lead some to lose all hope and others to write again; but the tone of their letters will clearly indicate who persists mistakenly.

*
* *

Well, I was mistaken. The seven true writers offered me their spiritual correspondence again, with the same finesse and equally beautiful phrases. Only the eighth, the refreshing gentleman with the torn page, has not given signs of life.

I almost laughed aloud alone. What is the good man thinking? He resents my silence, surely.

But if he suspected a supra-artistic correspondence, he would insist! Altogether, I believe I lost nothing.

*
* *

A month of correspondence! Did I truly seek to feed my soul with the magic word of the man of letters? Understanding, exquisiteness, anemic breath, ideal caress... my God! All, all that I possess of them! And I feel so, so empty!

After reading the seven letters consecutively, I always feel myself wholly, to the most intimate core of my being, something sweet; but almost imperceptibly so, of the slightest sweetness that turns yearning to be concretely sweet! I seem to float, unable to settle on earth. I touch things, and it is as if instead of suffering my touch, they flee. And in this state of flattened beatitude, I want to find myself! And this yearning for a definitive sweetness I will reach yet always escapes me!

Sometimes, after answering the seven letters, I think about the eccentric with the torn page. What would he have written? Unnamed vulgarities... but they would have made me laugh. Poor man! He still resents me.

And if I wrote to him again? Surely, he has never been so flattered.

***

Last night I sent him two lines. Here is his response:

Miss: You ask why I did not write to you again. I realized, after answering your letter, that I misunderstood. You spoke of a literary correspondence. And I am not a man of letters. Certain you will forgive my mistake, I send my rgds...

Not bad, no? Though he could have apologized for not being a man of letters: "... I realized *that*... forgive *my* mistake..."

But regardless of his ignorance, he must know what a literary correspondence is! To what end, since he played the fool at first, does he enclose himself in ferocious silence?

Oh! And the always poetic torn page.

***

What a dream! Last night I dreamt that a stranger knelt by my bed and whispered in my ear, "He's deceiving you. The others are men of letters; but he is a real writer."

The truth roughly revealed the reason for my concealed preference. Yes, doubtlessly! He dissimulates, his commercial style is a disguise! How did I not suspect it earlier? Now his attitude is wholly explained.

Oh, very well! Do not fear, gentleman writer. You are a bad psychologist, if you believe I will flatter your vanity, recognizing you as a poet!

*
* *

Mr.: Despite everything, be so kind as to waste time exchanging impressions with me? YOS would be greatly honored...

Miss: I cannot understand your interest in exchanging impressions since, as I said, I am not a man of letters. None of my impressions would entertain you. Believing I thus rightly satisfied your desires, I send my rgds...

*
* *

Oh, yes? So, sly gentleman of letters, you satisfied my desires just like that? Read this little letter:

Mr.: I too confess I briefly mistook you for a writer. With this double error, I terminate our ephemeral correspondence.

Only I erred. But he must be very skilled to reinitiate the correspondence triumphantly.

*
* *

And he does not resume! A month passes in obfuscated silence!

Did I make a mistake? Is he a common thug, without a breath of the ideal?

But no; he would have answered something spitefully crude, since the vanity of vulgar men, in their smallness, is stronger than that of men of letters.

So? What does he intend? To mock me?

I dreamt all night, waking at every moment. I am broken today, no taste for thinking of myself for an instant.

Leave it. I will resume correspondence with my seven true colleagues—writers after all. The other is dead.

*
* *

Mr.: Did you die? I ask, moved by the strictest curiosity.

He responds:

Miss: I am not dead yet. If in yesterday's little letter you wished to ask about my silence, I remind you that you imposed it, not me. Satisfied?

*
* *

Six hours later, he received the following single line from me: *I am not. Are you?*

And he, immediately: *Nor am I.*

**
* **

But such work! How hard it is to seduce him! My God! Is he this difficult to all the women who write to him?

"My" man of letters! In vain, his letters, style, and vulgarly clear explanations seek to fool me. Who, but an artist, could find the way to interest, not offend me? Vulgar men do not proceed this way. The eternally hungry without needs are like Maeterlinck's rich men.

**
* **

Two months spent writing to each other.

What does he tell me? I do not know. Nothing extraordinary. Oh, no! His same, constant, simulated simplicity. But how curious! His expressions, trivial coming from others, coming from him, the same words and tone, seem full of energy!

My man of letters! How I recognize your divine subtlety!

But his name, always a mystery. I exhausted the list of national writers, without finding his. Not a pseudonym either; I know him too well now to believe that. But, then?

Aunt laughed at my glumness yesterday.

"But aunt," I said. "He's a magnificent writer, I'm certain! And I want to read him!"

"And see him too, of course?"

"Of course, aunt!"

I updated her on his wish to meet me.

"Do you fear disappointment?" she asks.

"Why? I know he appreciates and respects me."

"And if he's ugly?"

"Very, very ugly?"

"Yes. And not a writer."

"Oh, aunt! That's impossible. You can't imitate a lack of literature to that extent, without being a man of letters... Ugly?... It doesn't matter. I'm not attractive either."

My aunt goes, "Um-hum... um-hum..." And concludes, "All right, Mechita: meet him. After ten minutes you'll know whether or not to continue your correspondence—a literary one."

"Yes, auntie! If not, I wouldn't be mad to meet him."

Tuesday, a big day!

Him

This afternoon at six on the dot, I will be at her door. Who would have guessed it four months ago, when I considered myself the most unhappy mortal because I could not find her? And now, waiting for me, reclining on thirty or so friendship letters...

I flew to tell her beloved aunt.

"Complete triumph!" I said, "She consents to see me."

"Congratulations! And knowing her spirit now, do you

like Mechita as before?"

"I'm mad. There's nothing more to say."

"Be clear: in love with her soul?..."

"Yes. For God's sake, ma'am! With her soul, yes! Despite her literary fetish, she has a sane mind. And her body also drives me mad."

"Don't repeat that. In short, be happy."

And I leave. I do not know what will become of me, when the fantasies she forged atop my artistic pastime come apart... Then we will see. But if it is true that she does not dislike me, as I am, and she is so terribly beautiful and pure as when standing in a salon, then, God, shield us!

Her

What a hallucination! Two hours of vertigo! I have the impression that I cried and laughed; I was struck down and sobbed with joy.

What joy! But how happy I am!

He left an hour ago. He arrived at six sharp and approached me with an irresistible frankness from the beginning.

My love! How to convey that your straight back conquered me before I touched your hand!

Without any variations, as I imagined him: dark-haired, no mustache, and a solid set of white teeth, very visible, when he laughs.

I think of my aunt's fear, "And if he's ugly?" I smile now.

Oh! But in the last quarter of an hour, after we talked and talked, and stood, and he looked at me, turning pale, and I had given him my soul already, ignorant to what he had done to me or how, oh, then I did not smile to myself, because I was sure I would die if he rested a finger on my shoulder!

My God! I rested my fainting head in his arms, when, as we said goodbye, he suddenly held me close!

Humiliation, pleasure, and horror for myself betrayed in my sobs. But above all I felt the immense protection of the hand that combed my hair and the support of the body that shielded me wholly.

While we were like this, he said nothing. And he will never know that his resolve to seduce me would not have made me as tenderly his as his immediate silence.

More than happy now! And how I laugh evoking the "tremendous catastrophe"! Do you remember the "vulgarity of men without artistic ideals" and the "crudeness of their feelings"?

Thus, I whispered to him, "Now tell me who you are, what books you've written."

He laughed, showing me more of his white teeth.

"It's just that I'm not a writer," he said. "But you dreamt... and I wasn't brave enough to disillusion you. I'm incapable of writing a single verse. I always had to work for a living; and all I can offer a woman is a strong...

prosaic heart."

Oh, what a speech!

Still laughing, he asks, "Do you love me like this... without literature?"

"With or without!"

"And," referring to my first letters, "a kiss is not a crude crime?"

"Oh, no!"

But he is about to painfully awake me, when he says, "We'll forget, then, that I was the beast; and you... I remember a children's story..."

"Yes, *La belle et la bête*..." I murmur in French.

But he adds, laughing, forgetting that I am convalescing, "That's it. I also know French, see: Donc, I am... la bête. Et you?"

My God! It's: et toi... But under his mouth I answer, fainting, "La bête, aussi!..."

Twilight

Carnival night in a fashionable seaside resort. The beach, two kilometers from the hotel, has become an oasis. Big palm trees, arranged in a rhombus, rise from the sand. The charity bazar is mounted on the shore, parallel to the sea. The tables among the plants offer bar service. In the small hours of the night in question, the party area—bazaar, palm trees, and sand—looks lonely under the galvanic radiance of the light bulbs.

Lonely, perhaps not, though, except for the buffet, the bazaar is in the dark, some people still defy the chilly-sea breeze in the palm oasis.

Three young men in tuxedos and two mature women, late night regulars of the bar, just sat down at a table quickly covered with bottles and cold cuts; and in even less time, their attention and eyes turn to a remote table, where a man and a woman, with nothing but an ice cream and a glass of water before them, sit across from each other, conversing.

He is a man of a certain age, older than his still youthfully handsome face would lead you to suppose. This man, years earlier, held a strong hold over women. He was not a womanizer. Though his conquests are never named, the danger he poses is certain. Better yet: that he posed.

She, the woman whose elbow rests on the table and

eyes are fixed on her interlocutor, is very young. A kid of sixteen. But the new arrivals will tell us all about her.

"There's the Dog of Olmos, trying to seduce Renouard," one of the ladies assesses.

"Dog?..." One of the young men asks.

"Yes, Lucila Olmos," explains the lady. "A family nickname... When she was little, she'd doggedly dig her heels in, refusing to have her arm twisted... Thus, her name."

"So beautiful, despite it..." The same young man comments.

"You better believe it! And she's put her beauty to good use... No, I'm not implying... She just returned from Europe. Poor ex-handsome Renouard, if the Dog decides to drive him up the wall."

"Is that her skill?"

"Oh, no! But she has a fixed style: doing what she mustn't. And she's too well-balanced, I always say, given how old her mother was when she had her, at least forty-five years old... Watch the immobile attention she pays to Renouard."

"Attractive..." Another young man murmurs, agreeing with the first.

"Yes, no one denies it..." The well-aware lady shrugs, "But not as young as you think..."

"But..."

"Yes, I know what you'll say... From your perspective, she's a child... She's just short of seventeen. But does age matter? The heart ages a woman. And do you know what the Dog of Olmos has done with her life? Almost nothing! Do you remember Saint-Rémy's concert two years ago? One night the maestro was playing at X's... suddenly the lights went out, no one knows how. During that brief darkness, Saint-Rémy felt a set of arms wrap around his neck and a mouth touch his. It lasted as long as a lightning bolt. When the light turned on again, Saint-Rémy was alone. And the woman closest to him, was meters away. During those scarce seconds of darkness, an unparallelly audacious woman traversed the empty space; she satisfied her passion for the musician's lips and escaped before the lights turned on.

Saint-Rémy continued his sonata as best he could. And when it was over and all us ladies went to congratulate him, the maestro scanned our eyes in vain, trying to discover the insecure gaze of his anonymous beloved.

Anyone would've felt unsettled. Not Lucila. She was the culprit. She'd just turned fifteen.

Do you realize the gall of a girl that age to do such a thing? And I say girl to say something, as the Dog has had that body and beauty since she was thirteen years old. Which she's made good use of, I say!"

"Tell us another story," someone else in the group begged.

"Another?!" the informed lady protested, "Ask your relatives. They may know more."

"So young...." Murmured the beggar.

"I said it before: on the cusp of seventeen. And already divorced."

"Huh?..."

"Yes, divorced. Oh, It's quite a story!... I'll put an end to the versions. Last year, all of Amsterdam awaited Else, the explorer returning from the pole, as one would the Messiah, all the women, both married and single, were crazy about him. The plane he was arriving in burst into flames and the hero emerged from the wreckage as a ghastly thing without eyes, without arms... The horror! His own mother, if she'd been alive, couldn't have faced him. Lucila married him."

"Chic!" a young man in the group exclaimed, turning to face the provoker.

"Yes, very chic," concluded the lady. "Two months later, she was divorced."

There was a long silence. In the too-cool breeze, under the hard blows of the sea, the muffled froufrou of the palm trees was audible, their crinkly shadows danced agitatedly on the sand.

Loud calls to the waiter and the next round conclude the topic for the seated group.

***

But at the remote little table our new acquaintances animatedly continue their conversation. They have been there for three hours, alone and absent from space and time, like people that finally find each other in this transitory life.

His hair was white and she, still in her cocoon. But to converse, understand, dream such an age difference means nothing, as the following proves.

"How old are you?" she had just asked him.

"Sixty well-lived years," Renouard answered, neither eagerly nor hesitantly.

"You don't seem it," the young woman observed, examining him carefully.

He gestured, running his hand through his still abundant hair.

"It's because of this," he said.

"No," she denied, shaking her head slowly. "It's because…" And added to end the back and forth, looking unwaveringly into his eyes, "… I feel it."

The man that posed a danger for any woman that got close to him, did not, at his age, mistake what that answer implied.

"You're an honorable girl," he offered with grave affection. Renouard fell silent. But later added, "You don't mistake what I mean, no?"

"I don't think so… The honor a dishonored woman retains, despite… Is that it?"

"That's it."

"And you, Renouard, don't mistake what my answer connotes?"

"Oh, no! You're..." Renouard stopped himself.

"What am I?" Lucila asks.

"Nothing. What I..."

"Renouard," interrupted the young woman, leaning on the table, "you used to be a ladies' man, no?"

Without answering the question, Renouard continued, "What I was saying, when you interrupted me, is that all of you—body, face, and way of being—resembles a person my memory of whom is, perhaps no longer beloved, but still infinitely painful. That person, if she still remembers me, could answer your question."

"The memory of the person I evoke pains you, but my own presence doesn't in anyway. Why?"

Renouard ran after the child's youthful radiance which imbued the cool nocturnal oasis with morbid tepidness.

"Why do I remember that person so? Because she's you," he murmured. And perhaps regretful, continued in a lighter tone, "Do you believe in the transmigration of souls among the living, Lucila?"

"Call me Dog."

"What?"

"Call me Dog. You called me Lucila. Call me Dog."

Between the melted ice cream and the empty water glass, the man rested his big, frank hand on the young woman's.

"Dog," he smiled.

The girl's features lost their embattled tension; satisfied, she pulled her hand away: "Now we'll always be friends."

"I'm yours already, Lucila."

"Dog."

"And hopefully…"

"No! Not hopefully! Dog!"

Under Renouard's white mane, a shadow cast life in his still young eyes. And fixing them on the young woman, as a man does, asked, "Do you know what you're doing?"

"Yes," she answered.

Another silence. Renouard broke it quietly, murmuring, "You're crime."

And she, almost inaudibly, answered, "I am."

Yet another silence, that no one broke this time. The group of young men and ladies left, abandoning a complete buffet service on the table. The sea sounded deeper, and the sand seemed whiter, colder, and more sterile.

Finally, Renouard laid both forearms on the table and began, "Before, I said you're the person you evoke, it's true. Witnessing a shard of life rise from the depths of one's past warps one's sense of time. That memory could answer to my pretense as a ladies' man. I've had the same luck as anyone, nothing else. But I doubt anyone keeps a stain like the one I owe to that memory. I gather someone told you about my conquests. Would you like me to share my failures? Can you hear something lurid?"

"Yes, if you tell me the whole story."

* *
*

"Listen. I was twenty or twenty-one years old. I seduced a woman too quickly. A woman..."

"Like me."

"Yes, but older. If I'd been older, I would've understood that curiosity, not love, threw her into my arms. My beloved observed my apparent composure with attentive mutism, my adolescent fatuity, my eagerness to make her happy: everything I surrendered to the spiritual creature that acquiesced to being loved by a vane yet pretty boy.

I was then a brazen youth, and that brazenness was my pride. So, I thought I misunderstood, while fastening my tie before the mirror, those words pronounced slowly:

'How eerie! I feel I wasn't with a man...'

I turned like lightning. She remained seated on the bed, her arms hung by her sides and her gaze was lost.

Understand? I was a strong boy. And having exhausted myself, the woman I loved dreamt, dissatisfied, that she hadn't been with a man...

But one has to be a man to value what that means. I barely understood it at that time. Later I appreciated the depth of that abyss of nullity in which I drowned before that woman. She was my lover that afternoon. Then, never looked at me again, as if I never existed for her."

Renouard grew quiet. In the distance of the palm trees frozen in dew, the waning moon emerged, incomplete, above the ocean. The young woman, mute too, remained in the same posture.

"Renouard," she called.

He turned to her.

"You said I look a lot like that woman. Is that true, Renouard?"

"Yes, she's you," he clamored. "Do you understand? Do you understand that I'd do anything to rid myself of the memory that her beauty, her body, exacerbate to the point of…"

"Take me."

Suddenly Renouard turned pale. She, pale too, watched him unflinchingly.

"Repeat what you said," Renouard murmured.

"It's easy," answered the young woman. "That memory tortures you? You said you'd give anything to rid yourself of it?"

"Yes."

"I'm yours. Take me."

"Lucila," the white-haired man bellowed with happiness. "Take me."

* * *

If after that offering, great enough to die of happiness; if that night, under the waning moon, the sixty-year-old man had shot himself for his good fortune, he would have fulfilled his life and duty with dignity. He did not or could not see his road to Damascus. Because hours later, with Lucila in his arms, he believed he reached the zenith of his fate, he felt his desperate impotence to entrust the young woman with an exhausted joy, it was hallucinatory, like a nightmare.

Like eight quinquennials ago, he found himself in the arms of a very beautiful child whose curiosity led her to the maddest generosity. As before, he turned to find her seated, her eyes lost in the void. And he heard, as the mother exclaimed forty years ago, before the insipid dawn of a boy, the daughter repeat, before his lamentable twilight, "How eerie! I feel I wasn't with a man..."

Translator's Note: Grazing Earth

The distorted awe with which Uruguayan author Horacio Quiroga (1878–1937) describes the Misiones Jungle is akin only to the way Jesuit missionaries and Spanish explorers wrote about the Argentine province before him. The flora and fauna are so minutely detailed that they are rendered hyperrealist, like the landscape of a mythical past or a science fiction future. Alvar Nuñez Cabeza de Vaca sought the white king of the Guaraní people in the sixteenth century. The missionaries evangelized thousands of Guaraní souls and constructed eleven settlements in the seventeenth century. The eighteenth century initiated the decadence of the Spanish Empire. In 1903, when Quiroga accompanied Leopoldo Lugones to the Jesuit-Guaraní settlement of San Ignacio Miní, the province has become a refugium peccatorum. They encountered houses, a school, church, and cemetery stripped to their scaffoldings and encircling a cross. This decaying sacred space physically represents the template of Quiroga's stories—characters retrospectively narrate how their current state of decadence resulted from an unassailable conviction of erred kindness. I have attempted to extract the thread of sanity and life in his illusory universe, but it escapes my grasp because it retracts from life towards death and madness.

Quiroga is best known for his collection of children stories, *Cuentos de la selva* (*Jungle Tales*), which is part of the primary school syllabi in Argentina. His stories, like all myths and fairy tales, depict events of such unjustifiable violence that magic must intervene as an avenging force to re-establish justice. His teachers were Edgar Allen Poe, Fyodor Dostoyevsky, and Anton Chekhov, writers whose power lies in creating characters so real they appear animate independently of their creator. However, empathetic justice rests not in physical transformation but in a specific mental metamorphosis that allows an animal or "alienado mental" (mentally alienated)—Quiroga's designation for the deceased or mad human being—to speak through the author. Borges famously said that Quiroga did badly what Kipling did well, their likeness is evidenced in their books with nearly the same title. I believe the Argentine critic was not suspect of the Uruguayan author's craft or originality but his ethics. He offers prophecies that transcend what is humanely imaginable. These visions can be easily misconceived as ways of escaping the present by deforming the future.

His narratives offer a fatal critique of colonialism and capitalism but no alternative. He depicts a modern society that banishes those that want to live otherwise—the mad, criminal, or indigenous—to marginal zones. In reference to Ursula K. Le Guin's *The Dispossessed*, Raymond

Williams claims, "a socially higher rather than a socially simplified form (. . .) is significantly only available in what is in effect a waste land." His literature is dangerous, it hypnotizes, sometimes even crosses over to a kind of evil that justifies crime. However, he seeks kindness for those to whom society refuses it. Not prejudice veiled with kindness. He holds no prejudice, at least in the limited range of his existence. Quiroga was not a traveler but a prisoner of the place that defined who he became. It is hard to see him in his multiple portraits. In one he stands next to Ana María Cires, his first wife. She died by suicide six years after they married. He burned most of her photographs. Cires holds him and keeps her gaze impassive. His head is tilted down but his eyes are looking forth, imposing distance and holding the viewer in place, apart from them. He held some at an imprisoning proximity and others at a threatening distance imposed by his seclusion.

The frontier between nature and civilization mirrored the threshold between life and death. To control nature was to placate madness. In the end he gave in to both but took death in his own hands. Quiroga ingested cyanide after being diagnosed with gastric cancer in 1935. Alfonsina Storni dedicated a poem to him when she heard of his death. The first line is "Morir como tú, Horacio, en tus cabales," (To die like you, Horacio, sanely,). She drowned at sea three years later. The affirmation of sanity in the face of death counters accusations of insanity he encountered throughout his life or proves that his approximations to madness prepared him to meet his end in a conscious rather than somnambulant state. Simone Weil completes her claim that flesh is the pretext of a false good necessary for sin stating, "I need God to take me by force, because, if death, doing away with the shield of the flesh, were to put me face to face with him, I should run away." For Quiroga illusion does not intervene between life and madness or death. Characters enter a hallucinatory state after their will has been transgressed. Only the fatal repercussions of violence on the body and mind, not the delusions of the transgressor, interest him. What surprises most about Quiroga's prose, both in his fiction and correspondence, is his pragmatism. When the narrator learns of a death or emerges from a hallucination, life continues without dwelling on what passed even if it might or will happen again. He felt God like Weil did, as a hunger and thirst, not a desire to be met.

His writing is simple and legible but perfect in ways that are hard to recognize at first. He untapped the potential of language, not as a poet—meaning encrypted in those words in that order—but as an oral storyteller—meaning encrypted in narrative structure so it can be retold in other words. In "Decálogo del perfecto cuentista" (Decalogue of the perfect storyteller) he instructs the aspiring writer to describe an event with only the immediately evident words. He is always sparse. A never-ending sentence halts before something too harsh to say with an exclamation point or ellipsis. He insinuates the worst truths to the reader. His characters enter an illusory state. Silence is not a lie but a gesture of respect towards the humanity of the character.

Quiroga attempted to broaden, not veil, reality through the inclusion of posthumous or non-human narration. He did not distort what he witnessed but tried to see more by allotting intentionality to all events and turning stories into myths. In "El regreso de anaconda" (The return of anaconda), he describes a snake guarding a dying man from other animals then being shot by hunters but not before laying its eggs by the corpse. The anthropomorphized animal attempts and fails to make sense of his fatal attachment to man. A disillusioned imagination serves self-knowledge instead of other ways of being in the world. It illuminates the surface of a well which reflects the observer's image but conceals its depth and *fondo* (ground). Life remains mysterious. In *Más allá* (*Beyond*), his last book, he describes characters that reach the limit of self-mythologization. They can no longer attribute intentionality to their own actions. The endings of these narratives do not circle back to the catalyzing action but fade as the narrators enter states they do not return from. Quiroga's last book is condemned to oblivion due to these open endings. This dilution of fiction until the unimaginable is reached. His characters are rid of their shields of flesh.

The stories that belong to his most renowned collections, *Cuentos de amor, de locura y de muerte* (Stories of love, madness, and death) and *Cuentos de la selva* (Jungle tales) have been translated into English and reordered into two collections published by University of Texas Press. *Más allá* (*Beyond*) remains untranslated and discredited. The eleven collected stories are set alternatingly in the jungle of Misiones and the city of Buenos Aires but in each one there is an undescribed third space entered before a gap of consciousness in the narration. "*Más allá*" (*Beyond*), the story the collection is titled after, and "Su Ausencia" (His Absence) are responses to Poe's "Berenice" and Shakespeare's *Romeo and Juliet*. What does Quiroga offer? His own breed of religiosity. A kind of faith in life even when you are half absent, half present in the afterlife or among nonhuman lifeforms. Like someone talking about an ancient scroll that has gone missing and of which the plot to be recounted orally has been forgotten, I can only describe the hold these stories continue to have on me. The awe the jungle inspired in him, and the ethics embedded in the preservation of life within it, is transposed to the humanity of the alienated individual. These characters range from a conductor that simultaneously leads and stops a train from crashing, and a father that seeks and finds his dead son but hallucinates that it is a hallucination, to a girl who dies to be with her lover but then parts from him to move from limbo into the afterlife. Each sees reality briefly before transcending eternally to the side of madness or death.

Through this alternation between losing and regaining consciousness, Quiroga recognizes how he was half absent from life before dying by suicide. To broaden reality so it includes posthumous and nonhuman narration was a valid but dangerous feat. The author, like the Jesuits that inhabited his beloved Misiones, lived with a hunger and thirst for an absence. They believed their desire would be met in the afterlife. He knew he would never be satisfied. *Beyond* is an admission that he erroneously sought truth at the threshold of death instead of the hearth of life. In "Las moscas" (The Flies), the moribund narrator is haunted by a hum that he identifies as pertaining to the flies hovering above him moments before he becomes, not a corpse, but one of them.

> From that same instant I acquire the clear and capital certainty that my life grazing earth awaits the instantaneity of a few seconds when it will extinguish itself entirely.
>
> This is the truth. Never has a more decisive one materialized in my mind. All the others float, dance in a distant reverberation of another *I*, in a past that does not belong to me either. My only perception of existence, as blatant as a blow delivered in silence, is that I will die an instant from now.

> But, when? What are the seconds and instants during which this exasperated conscience of living still courses through a placid corpse?

The narrator expends his last thoughts dwelling on the threshold between life and death. In various instances in this book characters are described as bodies "al ras de suelo" (grazing earth), not quite here or elsewhere. Quiroga was a man who felt alienated everywhere, except on his deathbed. These eleven stories narrate the instant of consciousness between life and death, stripped both of a description of the afterlife and the retelling of a life. *Beyond* is a feat as brave as dying in your right mind.

—*Elisa Taber*

HORACIO QUIROGA (1878–1937) was a Uruguayan author of short stories, novels, poems, and a play. He is perhaps best remembered for his *Cuentos de la selva* (Jungle tales, 1918) for children, which is still assigned in many schools. Quiroga was a master of blending the mystery and suspense of Poe with the particular strains of madness native to the jungles of South America with story collections like *Cuentos de amor de locura y de muerte* (Stories of love, madness, and death, 1917) and *La gallina degollada y otros cuentos* (The beheaded hen and other stories, 1925).

ELISA TABER writes and translates herself into an absent presence. *An Archipelago in a Landlocked Country* is her first book.

SUBLUNARY EDITIONS is a small, independent press based out of Seattle, Washington, publishing in the field of contemporaneous literature, i.e. writing unbounded by era or geography. A selection of our titles can be found below. You can learn more about us at sublunaryeditions.com

FALSTAFF: APOTHEOSIS / Pierre Senges, tr. Jacob Siefring
926 YEARS / Kyle Coma-Thompson, Tristan Foster
CORPSES / Vik Shirley
A LUMINOUS HISTORY OF THE PALM / Jessica Sequeira
THE WRECK OF THE LARGE GLASS / PALEÓDROMO / Mónica Belevan
UNDER THE SIGN OF THE LABYRINTH / Christina Tudor-Sideri
UNDULA / Bruno Schulz, tr. Frank Garrett
STUDIES OF SILHOUETTES / Pierre Senges, tr. Jacob Siefring
FRAGMENTS FROM A FOUND NOTEBOOK / Mihail Sebastian, tr. Christina Tudor-Sideri
TWO STORIES / Osvaldo Lamborghini, tr. Jessica Sequeira
THE VOICES & OTHER POEMS / Rainer Maria Rilke, tr. Kristofor Minta
THE POSTHUMOUS WORKS OF THOMAS PILASTER / Éric Chevillard, tr. Chris Clarke
A CAGE FOR EVERY CHILD / S. D. Chrostowska
MORSEL MAY SLEEP / Ellen Dillon
HOMECOMING / Magda Isanos, tr. Christina Tudor-Sideri
RATIONALISM / Douglas Luman
ANECDOTES / Heinrich von Kleist, tr. Matthew Spencer
[TITLE] / [Name of author]
LETTERS FROM MOM / Julio Cortázar, tr. Magdalena Edwards
WHAT THE MUGWIG HAS TO SAY & SILVALANDIA / Julio Cortázar, Julio Silva,
    tr. Chris Clarke
RABELAIS'S DOUGHNUTS / Pierre Senges, tr. Jacob Siefring
THE LIGHTED BURROW / Max Blecher, tr. Christina Tudor-Sideri
TRANSPARENT BODY & OTHER POEMS / Max Blecher, tr. Christina Tudor-Sideri
SHAMMAI WEITZ / Isaac Bashevis Singer, tr. Daniel Kennedy
A FRIEND OF THE FAMILY / Yves Ravey, tr. Emma Ramadan & Tom Roberge
BEYOND / Horacio Quiroga, tr. Elisa Taber
DISEMBODIED / Christina Tudor-Sideri
CHIMERAS / Daniela Cascella
MYSTERY TRAIN / Can Xue, tr. Natascha Bruce
THREE DREAMS / Jean Paul & Laurence Sterne
VAGARIES MALICIEUX / Djuna Barnes
THE LAST DAYS OF IMMANUEL KANT / Thomas De Quincey

MARIA WUTZ / Jean Paul
IF YOU HAD THREE HUSBANDS / Gertrude Stein
FANTASTICKS / Nicholas Breton
IVAN MOSCOW / Boris Pilnyak
POEMS / Karl Kraus
NEWTON'S BRAIN / Jakub Arbes
A LOOKING GLASSE FOR THE COURT / Antonio de Guevara
A CYPRESSE GROVE / Wlliam Drummond of Hawthornden
MORNING STAR / Ada Negri
ZORRILLA, THE POET / José Zorrilla
POEMS / Miguel de Unamuno
ESSAYS, PARADOXES, SOLILOQUIES / Miguel de Unamuno
JOAN OF ARC / Jules Michelet and Thomas De Quincey
PAGES FROM THE DIARY OF A JACKASS / Ante Dukić
PREFACES / Jean Paul
THE CITY OF DREADFUL NIGHT AND OTHER WRITINGS / James Thomson
THE COLLECTED WORKS / Kathleen Tankersley Young
EXERCISES / Benajmín Jarnés